The MIRACLE of MURLIN HEIGHTS

The MIRACLE of MURLIN HEIGHTS

by Clifton E. Snodgrass
with Wanda J. Herman

PITTSBURGH and COLFAX STS., SPRINGDALE, PA 15144

Printed in the United States of America
ISBN: 0-88368-073-4

Clifton E. Snodgrass
8913 North Dixie Drive
Dayton, Ohio 45414

Published by:

Whitaker House
Pittsburgh and Colfax Streets
Springdale, Pa. 15144

Some of the names in this book have been changed to protect the individuals involved. The events are as described.

All Scripture passages are from the King James Version.

CONTENTS

To
Wayne
without whose help I could never have
finished
and to
John, Robina, and Sandra
also
to
Carol
who helped greatly
and to all the saints at Murlin Heights.

FOREWORD

This is truly an inspiring and encouraging story of how a man with no formal training in the ministry was led step-by-step into fulfilling an important call for the Lord.

Clifton Snodgrass's personal encounters with angels, dreams, and visions are valid Christian experiences in dealing with an all-powerful, supernatural Heavenly Father. Brother Snodgrass can truly say with the Apostle Paul, "I was not disobedient unto the heavenly vision" (Acts 26:19).

"The Miracle of Murlin Heights" is a story which I believe many many people will identify with. The author grew up in a family poor in material goods but rich in the heritage of walking with God. His experience of seeking the Baptism in the Holy Spirit especially touched my life because my experience was so very similar.

This is one book I know will bless many lives ... because it gives all the glory to Jesus.

Jim Bakker
TV Host of the "PTL Club"

Chapter One

BRANDED

"Mommy! Mommy!" I tried to scream out. As my mouth framed the words, my voice refused to utter the sounds I so desperately struggled to form. My feet and hands felt like lead and my veins as though they were filled with ice; a numbing paralysis had settled over me as I struggled to return to consciousness from a deep sleep. Slowly, objects in the room swam into view—the iron bedstead, the tall bureau, other familiar objects that began to stand out against the blur of the darkness of the room I had been sleeping in. As I began to feel the blood warm my small body once again, at last I called out in desperation, "Mommy! Mommy!"

The curtain covering the doorway parted and the stream of light coming from the next room framed my mother's silhouette as she entered the room.

"What is it, Clifton?" I heard her skirts making a soft rustling sound as she moved swiftly toward my bed.

"What's the matter?" Her voice sounded tired and worried, as it well should be. My sister, Ruth, and I had contacted measles that spring and were both critically ill. As my mother sat down upon the feather-ticking mattress, I sat bolt upright and grabbed for her comforting form, for only her nearness could dispel the fear that I felt from the startling scene I had just witnessed.

I wrapped my arms around her, my heart throbbing in my throat, as feeling began to surge back into my trembling body, shaken with sobs.

"Oh, Mommy, Mommy," I cried.

"Tell me about it, honey," she said as she held me close and stroked my hair, reassuring me with her touch.

"Mommy, I just saw two angels come and get Ruth . . . and, oh, Mommy, they took her away. I saw them float up."

Mom held me away from her gently and said, "Are you sure now, Clifton? You were probably just dreaming."

As she talked, she put her hand against my forehead to see if I still had a fever.

I stated emphatically, "No, Mommy, I really saw it. They came and got Ruth."

Ruth was my baby sister, just two years younger than I. Though just barely two years old, she was such an intelligent child; it was she who had taught me how to talk. Now, her angelic face was covered with red spots and her curly brown hair lay limp and tousled from the perspiration of the fever of the sickness. Her usually sparkling brown eyes were fixed in a vacant stare.

It had been a hard winter that year and she and I had been sickly for some time. The drafty, three-room, shot-gun type house we lived in made the winter months very difficult. We had had more than our share of colds and flu. The cold chilly winds of winter would blow up through the rough floor of the hillside house which was supported by stilts on the downhill side. Now that spring had arrived, the measles had hit.

In the last day or so, Ruth had become increasingly worse, and so my mother and father had moved her into the other room. Just that evening when my father had returned home from working in the coal mines, Ruth came to greet him. He picked her frail little body up in his arms and she turned her eyes toward him so pitifully that he couldn't bear to look at her. He laid her down on the bed and walked outside the house weeping, his heart gripped with fear. Instead of recovering from the measles as a child normally would, she had developed complications and as the hill-folks of the Southwest Virginia area would diagnose it, they "went in on her."

I had grown sleepy and been put to bed for the night. My mother, the doctor, and some friends were gathered in the room with Ruth, praying for her recovery. My father, whose fear became great that he might lose both of his children, had gone to the woods to pray.

Now as my mother was speaking, her words failed to convince me that what I had seen was not real.

"But, Mommy, I really did see it! These two angels came and they had on shiny white dresses, and this light was all around them, and they got hold of Ruthie's hand... and, Mommy, she wasn't afraid of them either. She just looked at them and smiled. Then they all looked up at heaven and as they looked, they started floating up. I *did* see it. Ruth had on a white gown and it had ruffles on the bottom. I watched... I even saw her little feet hanging down from her gown. I watched them until they got too far for me to see."

At this moment, cries came from the other room, "Esther! Esther! Come quickly! It's Ruth!"

Hastily gathering me into her arms, she rushed into the room where my sister lay upon the bed, her tiny feet showing beneath the ruffle of her white gown. Stooping down over her still form, the words "She's gone!" broke the silence and wrenched forth an unutterable sob from my mother's anguished heart. Soon the room was filled with the wailing of those who shared her heartbreak.

When word of Ruth's passing reached my father, who still knelt in the woods agonizing in prayer, fear filled him for his only remaining child. Since the time of his conversion, God had called him to preach and he had steadily resisted the call. Now feeling that God was punishing him for his refusal to heed Him, he called out desperately in prayer, promising that if God would spare his son, he would preach the gospel. My recovery was assured.

A few days later, my mother and father sat amazed, recalling the vision God had given me of Ruth's passing, wondering why God had chosen to grant such a vision to such a small child.

As I look back to that winter of 1921, I realize it was the vision of seeing my baby sister Ruth carried into heaven by the angels that was burned deep into my mind and marked my memory with an indelible brand that would haunt me for years to come as I tried in vain to live the life that I chose for myself.

Chapter Two

INHERITANCE

From the time of my father's conversion, I was continually exposed to a succession of miracles. Although poor by most standards, the riches that my spirit accumulated was indeed a large cache. I hardly remember ever having more than one pair of shoes and since I needed those for church and special occasions, I attended school barefooted until the first snowfall, lest I scuff and mar that one pair beyond repair and be left with none. My bibbed overalls had "patches on top of the patches," and when I lost the buttons which held the top straps to the bib, I managed to fasten them with a nail. I never knew the luxury of excessive pairs of underclothes, thus in the summertime, my overalls, minus a shirt, were sufficient. When I joined the gang of boys at the old swimmin' hole all I had to do before jumping in was to "pull the nail," for even bathing suits were scarce in those days.

My father preached the gospel and lived the gospel. His faith was our example, and God kept our stomachs full, our backs warm, and a roof over our heads. Many times when a payment was needed or there was a lack of funds for the purchase of some necessary item, my father would go to his secret closet of prayer. Ultimately, a letter from some saintly soul would arrive, usually the day before the payment was due, stating, "Dear Brother Pat, the Lord has laid it upon my heart to send you the enclosed amount," and that check would be the exact sum sufficient for the need.

So, the inheritance that my father left me was not one of great material wealth, but of great spiritual wealth, gained through observing his ministry after his final yielding to the will of God. My father received his call to the ministry the night of his conversion.

It was the evening that "Blind Willy Thomas" stood in the midst of the small community church in West Norton, Virginia, his voice piercing through the exuberant praise of the people as they responded to the ministry of pioneer evangelist, Reverend Thomas Kidd. As "Blind Willy" spoke a divine utterance of God's judgment, fear fell upon all, both saint and sinner.

A strong sense of God's presence was felt by the congregation. The move of the Spirit of God brought a holy hush.

The only sounds heard were the muffled voices of excited neighbors on the outside as they exclaimed to one another, wondering at the mysterious light that was shining down on the roof of the church as brilliant as day. Just a few moments before, it had been so dark out that you couldn't see your hand before your face. Now, people were gathering around the building, and falling down on their knees to pray.

"Wonder what's going on in there?" someone was heard whispering.

Inside, the coal-oil lanterns shone forth as babes in arms and small children lay quietly on pallets at their parents' feet and watched their flickering lights cause strange shadows to play upon the walls and ceiling of the building. Then the silence inside was broken by choking sobs and a loud crash on the floor. Heads turned and the onlookers gasped in amazement.

Such fear had gripped my father's heart that his trembling legs had refused to carry him to the mourner's bench in front of the church. Sin's great weight of conviction forced him to the floor where he now lay sobbing and begging God for forgiveness. His buddies from the Odd Fellows Lodge, who had accompanied him for the purpose of disrupting the meeting, were awe-stricken.

My mother rushed back, giving praise to God, to kneel beside my father, and pray with him. She was beside herself with joy, not only was my father saved, but now she wouldn't have to face an angry husband on her return home from church.

Just before leaving for church that evening, she had withstood my father's angry threats.

"If you go down to that holy roller meeting," he had warned her in a voice filled with rage, "I'm gonna come in, drag you out, and beat you black and blue."

"I'm sorry, Pat, but I'm a-going and there ain't nothing you can do about it."

Quickly grasping her purse in one hand, swooping down and gathering Ruth in her other arm, she called to me, "Clifton, come here, it's time to leave."

She turned and faced my father's furious countenance. After exchanging determined glances, she rushed past him out the door and was soon on the way down the railroad track to the little country church two miles away.

As I trotted along behind her, we were soon joined by others on their way to the revival that gave birth to Pentecost in Southwest Virginia. What had started as a summer revival lasted nightly on through the winter into early spring, causing a great spiritual awakening in that area.

My father's anger demanded revenge against the preacher who he felt was responsible for creating a division in his home. At the meeting of the Odd Fellows Lodge that night, he saw an opportunity to recruit others who would join him in his vindictive actions.

"Boys, we're gonna go down there and tear up that church, whip that (blank-blank) preacher and run him out of town. Now all of you that are with me, we're gonna go in and sit in the back row. Wait for me to give the signal. When I say "NOW" we're really gonna give those fanatics something to carry on about. Just make sure you save the preacher for me."

By the time my father and his lodge brothers had arrived, the service was well under way. The enthusiastic singing was accompanied by guitar music, a couple of tambourines, and a whole lot of vigorous hand clapping as the people responded to the rhythm.

As the song came to an end and praises were scattered throughout the audience, my mother, sitting toward the front with Ruth and me, was one of the first to hear the commotion in the rear. Hard-soled work shoes rumbled on the floor as the men filed in to take their seats near the aisle. Now my mother, her heart heavy with dread, bowed her head and prayed quietly for God's protection.

The service continued, crescendoing in a roar of praise as hands were lifted and tears streamed down upturned faces. It was then that it happened. The heavenly message from "Blind Willy" broke through the din.

Realizing that the message was directed

toward him and his accomplices, my father rose to make his way to the wooden bench in front of the pulpit which faced the congregation and served as an altar. But God had other ideas. He now lay prostrate in the aisle with his buddies looking on, and all he could say was, "God, have mercy on me. I'm a sinner. Oh, God, save me, save me now."

It was while he was in this position of surrender, that he heard God speak audibly to his heart, *"I've called you to preach My gospel."*

Some of his friends also knelt that night and gave their hearts to God. But two of them, Uncle Lee, my father's youngest brother and Lee's brother-in-law, Clint Sloan, sat there in resistance. They felt the message was for them also, but each waited for the other to make the first move. This was typical of them as they did everything together, even to marrying twin sisters, working at the same jobs in the mines, and living in the same house.

It was after midnight when the final amen dismissed the congregation from the little building; but it did not dismiss the spirit of worship. Joy-filled saints, now including my father, and sleepy-eyed children trudged along darkened roads, passed occasionally by a horse-drawn vehicle carrying exhaltant saints, lost in worship. The radiance of their faces competed with the glow of hand-carried lanterns that bobbed alongside. An occasional shout of praise would echo down through the sleeping valley and bring a fresh awareness of the reality of God's visitation.

It was then, as they walked along, that my Uncle Lee confessed to my father, "Pat, I know that Clint and me should have been down there beside you praying, too, but I promised God that if I live until tomorrow night to get back to church, I'm gonna get saved."

My father slept little that night because of his new found joy and peace with God.

Before the sun rose the next day, he had already made his way into the mines through the drift-mouth, the main mine opening. The pony-drawn coal car which carried him and the other miners shuffled its way down the main heading to the room where his tools lay ready for a new day. There, from a kneeling position, he began to work the vein of 3-foot coal.

The work day was still young when a muted rumble was heard from a nearby "room" which sent icy chills through every miner who heard it. Soon thick coal dust filled the stagnant air like a black fog in the low room where my father worked. The small bare flame of the carbide light attached to his miner's cap barely penetrated the darkness as he made his way groping and choking toward the confusion of excited voices. There beneath the crumbled debris of fallen slate and rock lay the crushed bodies of Clint and Uncle Lee. As they had been together in life, so now they were together in death to face a God they had rejected less than twelve hours before.

Before leaving home that morning Uncle Lee had had a foreboding of an impending disaster. Not knowing it involved him, his last words as he left his wife, were, "Honey, I feel like somethin' bad's gonna happen today!"

This incident only served to warn my father of the danger of resisting God's will, although it wasn't until death had taken my sister Ruth that he finally yielded to the call to the ministry.

It was quite an exciting adventure for me as a young boy to travel with my Dad all around the Virginia countryside as he proclaimed the gospel of Jesus Christ to the simple mountain folk with a great burning zeal in his heart to be a "New Testament" preacher, a living member of the book of Acts.

My inheritance mounted up day by day until I had acquired a wealth of great lasting value. Every time things seemed to become commonplace, another outstanding event would transpire that would again implant its roots into my subconscious; events that would bear fruit later on in my life.

Not long after my eighth birthday, my

father, and his deacon, Brother Eck Fletcher, and I left on a Wednesday afternoon for Pardee, Virginia, a coal-mining camp on Black Mountain. Brother Fletcher and I often accompanied Dad on his speaking engagements. As we wound our way across the twisting road in our model "T," I felt the cold bite of the winter winds whip into my face through the open side window, where the curtains were missing. I snuggled close to the back of the front seat to keep the air from hitting full force upon me. I loved to go with my father when he went out, and the excitement of having this privilege helped to dispel any discomfort that I felt.

The church at Pardee was not pastored by any single individual. The church building was owned by the Pardee coal-mining company and served as a community building or union hall for whatever special occasion arose. As such, my father had the privilege of preaching there the fourth Wednesday of every month, the other Wednesdays being rotated in turn by the Baptist, Methodist and Presbyterian preachers.

Upon arrival, as the car chugged its way to the side of the church and came to a stop, I strained impatiently against the seat of the car, eager to be out with the other boys I saw scampering around the churchyard.

"Brother Pat, something seems wrong. Look at the people's faces. They don't seem quite so happy to see us. Wonder what's happenin'?" The deacon's voice was filled with anxiety.

My father's eyes scanned the faces of the people who were milling around outside, but he spoke with confidence. "If there is a problem, no matter what it is, God knows all about it and can take care of it, Eck."

As he opened the door, I slid out past him and made my way over to the nearest group of boys, but before I could barely say my first hellos, my father's voice called out to me, "Come on, Clifton. I'ts time to be going inside."

Reluctantly, I followed Dad down the aisle where I was motioned to my place on the front pew, while he continued toward the platform. He had scarcely reached the pulpit when a commotion was heard outside. Brother Eck looked toward the door with concern, but my father, as was his habit upon arriving at a church, turned and knelt at the bench setting on the rear of the platform. He began to call upon God for His help in the forthcoming service. Brother Eck glanced again toward the door, then he too fell upon his knees in prayer, following my father's example of "committing all to God."

I sat there, absorbed in swinging my legs back and forth under the seat, impatient at having to wait alone. Then the angry shuffle of feet and the loud murmur of disapproving voices brought me to full attention. Something was going to happen, and that "happening" was headed right up the aisle coming closer to the platform with each step.

I turned and with surprise noted a Blackwood policeman in full uniform headed up the aisle where Daddy was praying. He stopped short at the platform, hesitated for a moment, then called, "Hey, preacher!"

Up until this point, my father had seemed oblivious to all the commotion, intently communicating with his Maker. Now he turned his head to see who had called him.

As the sheriff noted the glow upon his face, it seemed to throw him off guard for a moment; he was not quite sure how to react to someone who looked as if they had just been speaking face-to-face with God.

Daddy slowly rose from his knees to a standing position to face the burly policeman. Brother Eck got up also and came to stand beside my father. It seemed as if the whole congregation moved silently forward and pressed together as if to hear all the better. I felt this, rather than actually seeing it, for my eyes were glued upon the unfriendly face of the sheriff.

My father's voice spoke out of the silence. "You speaking to me, sheriff?"

"Yeah, preacher, 'fraid I am. I came to tell you that you gotta close this meetin' down and move along. Ain't gonna allow you to have no more meetin's here in this town. We all," with this he swung his hand to take in all the observers, "want you to get out and *now*! Ain't no *holy rollers* allowed in here no more."

As my father stood there, his eyes searched the crowd, letting it register in his mind that what he had heard was true.

I was instantly filled with scorn for these people. "What's the matter with them?" I thought. "Don't they know my daddy ain't never done nothin' wrong? Don't they know how good he is?"

A swift glance from my father, showed that he perceived my thoughts. Flushed with embarrassment, I dropped my head. I began to pray within myself, not really knowing what to pray for, "God, help us, whatever we need. Don't let them treat us like this."

I don't know whether my prayer helped or not, but at that moment the Spirit of God moved in upon the scene. A look of boldness came over my father and Brother Eck's faces as they moved down the aisle making their way through the crowd. Their voices began to break forth in praises to God in the midst of those self-willed people. I hung onto my father's coattail not sure of what to do. As the Spirit moved upon him, it was then that he became the "master of the situation" instead of the "unsure servant."

He and Brother Eck moved as one. At the same moment, they began to wipe their feet on the steps of the church, as Jesus had told His diciples to do in Luke 9:5 when *they* were not received.

"This place shall not prosper," spoke my father, "for you have not just rejected us, you have rejected the Lord."

The spirit of the crowd was broken, and each person looked at another trying to determine just what their reactions should be now. Here and there a few people dropped their heads shamefully, realizing that a pronouncement of doom had fallen upon them. They were unsure of what to do next.

As we climbed into the car and it sputtered to a start, Daddy was still magnifying and praising God for the situation; that they had been counted worthy to suffer for His name.

"Eck," I heard him say, "God's Word says, 'blessed are ye, when men shall revile you and persecute you...for My sake'" (Matthew 5:11).

As I watched the crowd vanish from view as we rounded the curve, I turned around and sat back in the seat. I felt daddy's elation would soon die down, he would come to himself, and everything would be back to normal. But little did I realize that God was about to manifest His glory and miraculous power to His servants in reward for the New Testament action they had taken.

"Praise the Lord," Brother Eck sang out, "Praise the Lord!"

"Praise the Lord!" my father responded with equal fervor.

As their praises rang out magnifying and glorifying God, their English tongue (with its Virginia dialect) changed to a language that made no sense to me. It was a language I had often heard when they "got happy" and "got in the Spirit." Both men raised their hands in the air simultaneously as a gesture of thanksgiving that they were counted worthy to be used in His service.

As the car continued chugging its way down the narrow, winding, blacktop road, full of sharp turns, I thought, "Oh, no! Daddy's gonna wreck this car if he don't get a-hold of the steering wheel."

"Daddy!" I yelled, "Eck! Look out! We're gonna wreck!"

But they were oblivious to all and lost in a spirit of worship. Though screaming at the top of my voice, my words were overpowered by the exuberant praise combined with the noise of the engine.

Looking out over the short hood of the model "T" and down the road as it wound its way down the side of the mountain, with its deep ravines on one side and rock walls on the other, my heart seemed to choke in my throat so that no other words could escape. Turning to the window, I stared in horror. As the trees alongside passed in a blur, I looked down into the valley where the peaceful scene of a gently flowing creek seemed to contrast with the terror I felt inside the car—the terror of an imminent crash.

All my senses were alerted and seemed to demand immediate action. My first thought was to hide on the floor and cover my eyes so that I couldn't see the road and wouldn't know the exact moment of the crash. My next impulse was to take control of the car myself. Quickly I made an attempt to reach between the two men in the front seat and grasp the steering wheel which now seemed to be turning lazily of its own accord.

As I lunged forward, I was knocked into the back seat again by their waving arms.

Around each curve we went, the men in the front shouting, with uplifted arms and closed eyes, while in the back I regained my bearing and once again attempted to reach the steering wheel. But, again I was met by a barrier of praising arms, and immediately found myself helplessly lying on the back seat. Further attempts also proved futile as the car continued on the trip down the mountainside toward the next little mining town of Dunbar.

"What'll I do?" I thought desperately. Panic grew inside me and my stomach had a sinking feeling as I watched that wheel turn, and then looked ahead to the big curve coming into view. A picture formed in my mind of the car not making this next turn of the road and plunging into the yawning ravine which seemed to be just waiting to swallow us.

I sat there helplessly as the car rounded the curve that unforgettable day. I don't really know the moment the realization came, but slowly my mind began to absorb the fact that although no human hands touched the wheel, that car made each turn and twist perfectly down that mountainside!

Yes, God was with us and sent His angel to drive our car that night. When we got to Dunbar and Brother Eck and my father came to themselves and realized what had happened, it was enough to set them off again, and I was a long time getting home that night.

It wasn't until sometime later that I realized another miracle had occurred that same time—one of prophetic judgment. The word soon got out that the church at Pardee which was closed that evening to those who would preach the full gospel was never opened for another service. As my father had "wiped his feet" symbolically, so had God literally "wiped His feet" of a hard-hearted people. They had rejected Him once too often.

Later in life, when I had become a pastor, I thought about this incident, and determined to see for myself if the old church was still there and if it was being used or not.

One summer day, when my wife and I were vacationing for a few days in Virginia, visiting her folks, I decided to make that trip up to Pardee.

There on that same spot stood the old building—but what a difference since that memorable day in 1926.

The scene that met my eyes was evidence of God's judgment. I don't know why they allowed such an eyesore to remain to detract from the landscape. It's weather-beaten shake shingles from the roof lay scattered throughout the churchyard. Gaping holes in the roof allowed the weather to assault the interior at its own will. It sagged at the seams and seemed ready to crumble at the slightest disturbance. Its eaves now offered sanctuary to creatures of nature. Weeds grew in profusion. Some pews had been carried outside and sat rotting from exposure to the extremities of the changing seasons.

I pulled up, parked, and got out. As I strode over and peered into the windows, I stared in amazement. The floors that once supported rejoicing saints now could hardly afford to support the dust of their memories. All remains lay in a shambles.

As I pulled away from that place 45 years later, God's presence came down and surrounded me. His voice seemed to say, "Son, you've seen the evidence of My power. You, too, can have this same anointing."

My heart felt as though it would burst out of my chest with the fullness of His Presence. I replied, "Yes, Lord, I want it. I want it!"

Then all the experiences of that day flooded my memory and I decided to measure the exact distance that God's angel had driven our car. I followed the twisting, turning, serpentine road, remembering vividly each detail of the ride. When I pulled up to the town's bridge spanning the small creek, my speedometer registered one and a half miles. Although short in distance, it remains in my memory, the longest ride in my life.

Chapter Three

THE GLORY BARN

By the time I was eight years of age, my father was a full-time pastor and had gained considerable recognition for himself. He was overseer of a three-state district for the Assemblies of God. His district included Southwest Virginia, Eastern Kentucky, and Southern West Virginia. His pastorate consisted of four churches. He visited each of these one Sunday out of each month. In his absence, the care of the church was left to a head deacon.

Although absent from the individual congregation for weeks at a time, his close relationship to the Lord kept him aware of every secret situation. Nothing passed him by.

Upon arrival at each church, a business meeting would be held prior to the service. It was then that Dad produced a little black book, whose appearance provoked curiosity to the innocent and trembling fear to the guilty, for his word of knowledge ministry was known by all members.

"Sister Miller," he would begin, "the Lord showed me that on January 9th, you told a lie on Sister Kelly to try and make her leave the church."

He never had to ask if it were true, for the revelation from the Lord was so accurate and descriptive that no protest could arise from the lips of the guilty one. Repentance was immediate and revival resulted.

And so the visits to each of his pastorates would bring swift correction along with spiritual exhortation and a deepening love for God's power. At the same time many souls were won for the kingdom of God.

The biggest event of the week for a preacher's family was, of course, going to church. Our lives had become church centered. Church provided our religious education, social activity and our entertainment. Some might think we would have grown bored with having to attend church so often, but not so in my father's circle of ministry. Something unusual and often miraculous was bound to happen.

One of the most outstanding miracles I stored in the treasure chest of my memory took place at a revival in the old "Glory Barn" in the little town of Big Stone Gap, Virginia, a community about twelve miles from where we lived in Norton.

The building, donated by Mr. and Mrs. Taylor, who owned the adjoining property, was once an unused barn, which had been converted into a place of worship.

This donation was a result of the prayers of the people of Big Stone Gap, who wanted to attend a full-gospel church but had to drive several miles away to a church further up the valley where my father pastored.

When their willingness to offer this building as a church was made known, my father found that he had another congregation.

Because of its construction it easily held large crowds, and evangelists, such as James Hamil (who met and married my father's piano player) and Otto Lunsford, filled it to capacity, preaching old-time gospel with signs following their ministry. I personally saw the blind see, the deaf hear, the dumb talk, large goiters disappear and short limbs grow to full length. Because of these and other miraculous happenings, it had rightfully earned for itself the name of the "Glory Barn."

People came in spite of the totally alien appearance of the church building. Each uncomfortable bench was made by laying a rough-hewn plank across two logs; it still maintained its dirt floor which had been packed smooth by the feet of the many people who frequently jammed the building for the worship services.

On this particular evening the service was about to begin. Some worshipers were already seated. Others mingled in the aisles greeting fellow Christians. Their voices, mixed together with the noise of the musicians on the platform tuning up, created a cacophany of sound.

The naked electric bulbs, hanging in their sockets by a thin wire from the rafters overhead, scattered their sparse light about, dispelling the darkness in the cavernous building. I made my way onto the platform to ask permission to sit with my friends in the rear. The crudely constructed platform, with its cracks so wide they challenged any young boy to spit through them, squeaked and creaked as I walked to where my father sat leafing through his Bible.

Having received my orders on church behavior, I had no sooner sat down with my buddies when the song leader stepped forward to open with prayer and announce the song.

Joyous singing filled the air, "There's going to be a meeting in the air in the sweet, sweet bye and bye..."

Clapping hands picked up the rhythm and here and there some feet kept a tapping pace. The songs were accentuated and punctuated with enthusiastic "amens" and "halleujahs."

It wasn't long before some of the people began dancing up and down the aisles, eyes closed, arms stretched upward, oblivious to those around them. They were following the leading of King David in 2 Samuel 6:14; for David "danced before the Lord with all his might."

I looked up to see a group of people enter the building and take their seats about halfway down the aisle. Among them, I noted, was a cousin of mine. I was mildly surprised for his family was not known as church-goers.

I sat there smiling to myself, enjoying the scene which met my eyes, until suddenly what I saw filled me with indignation and caused a red flush to creep up from beneath my collar.

There sat my cousin and his group mocking the worshipers. Observance of those around them produced a mimicry that was not motivated by the Spirit. They pretended to jerk, shake, and move their mouths in jabbering words as if they were "speaking in tongues" and were "in the Spirit," then, they would turn to one another for approval. This would produce an instantaneous outbreak of giggles and smothered laughter. I realized as I sat a few rows behind them that they had not come to worship, but only to have a few laughs at the expense of God's children.

People nearby began to turn and stare, becoming agitated and upset by the disturbance, but not really knowing what to do. I noted that some of them dropped their heads in prayer concerning the disrespectful behaviour.

As the service progressed, each portion of the meeting, with its various participants, would provoke that group of irreverent men and women to further imitate the actions of what they called the "holy rollers." I wondered what my father would do when it came his turn to preach if they kept this action up. Would he denounce them from the pulpit, proclaiming them as an abomination in God's house?

But instead, when his turn came, he arose, read his text and began to fervently and mightly preach the Word. The power of the Holy Spirit became a hovering Presence, unseen, but felt by all. It seemed to envelop my father and add its weight to his words.

As my father preached with his usual zeal, his deep Virginia voice resounded throughout the building, filling it with his anointed message. I could always tell when he began to "feel the Spirit," for as his words became more rapid each phrase was finalized with a gusty "huh-uh" followed by an upward heaving of the shoulders as his head snapped back and his mouth opened wide to gulp enough fresh air to sustain the next powerful utterance.

Soon his coat was hastily removed and flung with abandon to a nearby empty folding chair, landing in a crumpled heap.

He rolled his shirt-sleeves up past his

elbows to give more freedom to his articulate gesturing as he emphasized each phrase. His tie was hanging loosely about his now unbuttoned collar, perspiration streaming from his brow, reflecting the light of the bare bulb hanging just overhead. His white shirt looked like he had just come in from a rain shower.

His already soaked handkerchief, snatched from his hip pocket, mopped his forehead.

The audience was caught in the spell. Shouts of "amen" followed each positive statement.

I looked all around the building and noted the mood of the crowd, and saw that even the eyes of that unbelieving group seemed riveted upon my father, but not without sneers of contempt upon the faces of a few. I thought to myself, "It'd serve them right if God would pronounce judgment on them."

These thoughts had scarcely entered my mind when I heard gasps hiss through the audience. I looked up to see people rising to their feet and moving to the center of the aisle where a woman had collapsed on the floor.

"She's dead!" someone cried.

I sucked in my breath as the shock ran through me. The whole audience seemed to rise to their feet as one.

The woman who now lay lifeless had come with the group that had just previously been mocking the power of God. She had been sitting on the end of the pew and had just toppled over into the aisle. Those gathered around her checked her pulse, trying in every way to see if they could determine if life still existed in the still form, but it seemed of no avail.

All eyes now turned to my father, who had kept right on preaching.

"Brother Pat, she's dead!" someone yelled.

But my father kept right on preaching to the amazement of the congregation. The situation at hand did not deter him from his duty. He always believed in moving *in* the Spirit, not *ahead* of Him.

Then suddenly, while still preaching, he stepped down from the pulpit, his full weight causing a stirring of the dust on the floor. He hastily moved toward the place where the dead woman was lying. The people cluttering the aisles parted to make a path for him.

Suddenly, he stopped several feet away, and with his left hand raised to heaven, his right hand thrust forward, his forefinger pointed at the woman, and with a voice that seemed to shake the very rafters, he thundered, "I say unto you, in the name of Jesus, rise up and walk."

Excitement, mixed with disbelief, caused a murmur to ripple throughout the crowd at his bold command.

Suddenly, before our very eyes, the quickening power of God began to bring life back into the seemingly lifeless form. As movement was detected, frightened children clung to their awestricken parents. Tears streamed down the faces of both saints and sinners as sinners knelt to pray and saints began to rejoice while the woman stood to her feet.

So much dancing and rejoicing took place that I could no longer see anything else from my short height.

Needless to say, a revival broke forth that lasted for some time to come, and it spread across the countryside and won many souls to the kingdom of God.

Such was my heritage.

Chapter Four

THE DECLINE

The road that lead to my conversion was downhill all the way. As I grew older, I, like the prodigal son in Luke 15:11-32, was determined to leave my home with its strict morality and old-fashioned holiness standard, and seek out a way of life that would be one of my own choosing.

Although faithful in church attendance, sometimes unwillingly, and seeing the continuous parade of miracles and healings, it wasn't until age fourteen that I saw my own spiritual need, but then it was an experiment rather than an experience. Perhaps I felt guilty. As the son of a preacher and a musician in the services, I sometimes felt people expected it of me. But, being the son of a preacher and continual church attendance did not make me exempt to the temptations of boys of that age.

Having yielded one night to the real conviction that I was a terrible sinner, and sincerely praying at the altar for forgiveness, my salvation experience had not progressed very far when I began to succumb to those boyhood temptations. And, my actions left me with so much guilt that I no longer had any joy.

Thus, when at age sixteen the opportunity to drive a beer truck came along, coupled with the promise of an increase in my financial status, I jumped at the chance. Even though my family disapproved, I knew they needed the extra income and I felt that I needed the prestige of being on my own. Of course, this job kept me away from church and exposed me more and more to the excitement and "glamour" of cities like Cincinnati and Chicago.

The little time I now spent at home was easier, for I was on the road driving my truck much of the time and did not have to listen to constant lectures from my parents.

This was not my first experience of being away from home, however. I had been as far away as Florida. A friend and I had run away together. We were both fourteen, and between us we had fifteen dollars and thought ourselves rich. Careless spending soon dwindled our fortune to the place that we had to choose between working or starving.

After working two weeks in an orange grove

for fifty cents a day, the thoughts of home began to beckon.

Catching the first freight train north, I was soon on my way back. Part of the way I had to hitchhike, but the last fifty miles, I just hiked.

Arriving home hungry, dirty and exhausted, I met Dad on the front porch.

"I've come home to die, Dad."

"No, son," Dad replied with an all-knowing look, "you didn't come home to die, you just came home to eat."

But soon after returning home, I forgot the fear and worry of being out alone and my thirst for adventure returned.

Now, serving God was the farthest thing from my mind. The one thing that *was* on my mind was girls, and with my job, I purchased a 1930 Ford convertible for sixty-five dollars. Few young men had a car in those days, so girls became as plentiful as bees swarming around a hive.

I felt I was all set for life. I refused to think about spiritual things anymore, and determined not to be obligated to attend church unless I chose to. I did like to go, though, for it gave me a chance to play my new guitar and meet more girls.

Before I had become restless and gone out on my own, Dad used to take my cousin, "Happy" Simpson, and me along with him to be the special singers before he preached. We earned the name of the "Halleujah Boys."

Thinking back to that time when we used to sing and play together, I realize that it was then that I first felt what it was like to be anointed by the Holy Spirit in service for the Lord.

It was one of those nights as I was playing on an old, three-dollar Sears and Roebuck guitar that the power of the Lord fell in a special way; it was as though the strings of my guitar were made of water. I couldn't feel a thing . . . it was marvelous . . . my fingers flew from chord to chord, all on their own. From time to time I would receive this special anointing and even the audience seemed to sense it.

But I had come a long way from those experiences. Now I played and watched the girls to see which one I wanted to take home that night after the service. Things of the spirit fled my mind and the void was filled with things of the flesh.

It was in a church in Appalachia, Virginia, where I met Beulah. I had just arrived home from one of my runs on the truck and impulsively decided to attend church that night where my Dad was going to be the special speaker. I thought I might even see some new girl.

I was especially proud of the new outfit I had just bought with my hard-earned money, for I felt it would make just the right impression.

Church was already under way when I made my entrance. I swaggered up the aisle with my spanking new black guitar slung back across my shoulder, trying to appear nonchalant in my black leather jacket. I felt it went well with my black riding breeches and black knee-high boots with their lacings crisscrossing up the front.

As I took my seat upon the platform with the other musicians, I noted a girl I had taken home several times before sitting a couple of rows back. She caught my eye and smiled, but it was the girl seated beside her that stirred my interest. She was partially blocked from my line of view by an old pot-bellied stove. I kept trying to peek around it, without being too obvious, to get a good look. I had never seen her before. As I strained to get a better view, the other girl assumed I was trying to get her attention.

At first that didn't bother me too much, for that way I could flirt with both. Then I saw her lean towards Beulah (as I later found her name to be) and I read her lips, "I just know he's gonna ask to take me home tonight."

The rest of the service is still a complete mystery to me for the only thing I remember is thinking, "How am I gonna get rid of her and get to meet this new girl?"

The moment the final amen was pronounced, I made a dash for the outside where I wouldn't be seen talking to the first girl by the new girl. I made my excuses and waited.

She had attended church with her grandmother and now waited inside with her until the people they rode with were ready to leave, which seemed to take forever.

When she finally appeared in the doorway, I stooped forward and introduced myself.

"Hi there, I'm Clifton Snodgrass. What's your name?" I tried my best to be suave to impress her.

"I'm Beulah Gardner."

I saw her grandmother make her way toward the car they came in and figured I'd better work fast.

"I know you've never seen me before, but I'm the preacher's son, and I, uh, I thought maybe, uh, you might allow me to drive you home."

"No thanks," she replied haughtily, "I don't go riding with strange boys."

Well, that just about floored me. I'd never been turned down before.

"Well, maybe next time," I stuttered, not quite so sure of myself.

"Maybe," she replied flippantly, giving me a half-smile as she turned away to join the others.

She intrigued me. The thing that attracted me most about her was her arrogant independence. I thought about her all the next day and wondered if she would be at service again that night. I broke my record and decided to attend two nights in a row.

I didn't know it, but she finagled a way to get back to church just to see me again. She refused to let me take her home, but did allow me to make a date to come and see her.

After a brief courtship, we were married. And, our marriage did *not* include religion.

I soon found another outlet for my talent of playing the guitar. Some of my new worldly friends were musicians also, and we formed a hillbilly band. We entertained at many social gatherings. While we played music, Beulah would bring down the house with her tap dancing act dressed in a sloppy print dress, hair bound up in a bandana scarf and her face painted black.

In the years that followed, God was not a part of my life at all. It seemed I had done quite well on my own.

I had a good job; a new car in my driveway; a new truck to deliver the wholesale pastries which I sold to groceries and supermarkets. My family was well cared for in the home I had recently purchased, and our only child, Wanda, was doing very well in high school. Yes, I felt that I had done quite well.

But just like the walls of Jericho, it all crumbled down.

I sat dumbfounded in the doctor's office trying to absorb the impact of his words.

Sitting on the examination table stripped to the waist, the words whirled through my mind.

"Mr. Snodgrass, you will never work another day in your life."

"How can he mean that? This can't be real. Surely I'm dreaming." Troubled thoughts rose up and perplexed my mind.

"Surely, Doctor, you can't mean what you are saying?" I pleaded, questioning his diagnosis. "What about my family? We have to live on something. I have to work!" By now my voice had risen to a high pitch.

Gently, the doctor placed his hand on my shoulder to calm me down. "I'm sorry, but I do mean it. Your heart is working too hard; it needs a rest. Your weight is causing too great a strain. You cannot continue to perform the kind of work you're doing, especially the lifting and the hours that you're keeping."

"Isn't there anything I can do?" I earnestly probed his face for some visible sign that he would soften his verdict.

"Well, it will be hard, but first of all, you must get as much of that excess weight off as quickly as possible." Then with a stern look of reproach he said, "I would advise you to get a desk job and just be a supervisor."

It sounded impossible! But, nonetheless, I

left that office with a determined, although grim outlook. I had to take action. I drove around, my mind calculating all the possible solutions. I looked again and again at my watch, knowing I must soon return home and face my wife and daughter with the situation.

It was too late to regret that I had put off seeing the doctor when I had first noticed the signs.

"Well, that's it!" I said with a finality.

I could see the stunned look in Beulah's eyes. "But Cliff, sell the business! Isn't that rather drastic? Maybe you shouldn't be so hasty."

"What else can I do?" I leaned forward to rest against the table, feeling that tired dull ache in my chest which was now quite familiar.

"I suppose we don't have much choice." She moved over to where I sat and put her arms across my shoulder trying to comfort me. "Something will turn up. It'll all work out, I'm sure."

"Hey, how about that, doc." I swung around to look triumphantly in his face. "Didn't think I would do it, now did you?"

"Pretty good. Thirty-five pounds in thirty-five days, but you can't continue to lose this fast. You'll have to take it a little slower now. It will help to lose some more weight, but you still *must* take it easy."

"I know. I've already sold my business. It looks as if the house is sold. I've purchased a bottling plant in Tennessee. All I'm going to do is supervise." I was elated, for my worry as to how I would provide for my family had been relieved. I felt as if all my problems had been solved.

Not only that, but Kingsport, Tennessee, where we would soon be living was only about thirty miles from Big Stone Gap, Virginia. This had pleased my wife for we would be close to both of our families and there wouldn't be those long trips when we wanted to go home to visit them.

"Perhaps this has all worked out for the best after all," I contemplated while driving home. *This* drive home from the doctor's office brought quite a different analysis than the one just one short month ago.

Did I say all I would be doing was supervising? I had bought the business, sight unseen. When we had called home to tell our families the news of my illness, my brother-in-law told me of a business opportunity he had just heard about.

I believe the words he used were, "You'll make a killing at it."

I pictured myself sitting at a desk, issuing orders, not lifting anything heavier than a pencil. I soon found that I had jumped from the frying pan into the fire.

My venture into his new field of business had been poorly timed. The ink was hardly dry on the purchase contract when the two major bottlers, Pepsi Cola and Coca-Cola engaged in a price war. I soon found that I could not compete with them, because to sell at their prices I would be losing money on every bottle I sold.

"Just look at me now," I muttered to myself while slinging a case of empty pop bottles back onto the truck. At the time of purchase, men to do the job of delivery had been the farthest thing from my mind. Now they were the *only* thing on my mind—finding them and being able to pay them.

"Here I am, doing work that is three times harder than what I had done in Ohio and worrying twice as much."

To be able to pay the few men I had, I kept back some of my own checks without cashing them, so it was getting to be even harder to provide for my family.

Now Wanda's high school graduation was near and she had firmly asserted that she had never been happy in Tennessee and as soon as she graduated, she was leaving to return to Dayton, Ohio.

My wife and I were having our own

difficulties because of the financial pressure and she kept threatening to return home to her mother.

"There's just so much that any one man can take," I resolutely spoke aloud as I climbed into the truck and slammed the door. "God, I can't go on any longer!"

The words echoed in my mind. Whose name did I just say? God! Where was *He*? How long had it been since I had spoken His name in prayer? I had tried so hard to keep Him out of my life.

I had tried to live my life to its fullest, becoming involved in everything I came in contact with until there was no time left in any day for God... but then the nights, that was different; the nights belonged to Him. Those I couldn't control.

Hardly one night had passed since I began my downhill road that I didn't wake up scared and shivering, the vividness of what I saw still framing my vision. I had to sweep away the cobwebs of sleep and rouse completely before I could rid myself of that intrusion that never failed to remind me of that long ago night when the angels had come to take Ruth away. It was real enough at night, but each morning I would push it back into the hidden closet of my mind.

Now, I drove back to the bottling plant, wearily turned out the lights and closed and locked the door to the office for the weekend. I walked slowly out into the dimly lit loading area. While standing there, a great sense of loneliness swept over me. An emptiness filled my heart as vast as the warehouse I now stood in. Tears began to trickle down my cheeks falling in drops that wet the concrete floor below.

"God, how can I call upon you? I've forgotten you for so long." The emptiness was replaced with guilt. My downhill road had finally reached the bottom.

It was Saturday night. I looked swiftly at my watch. Maybe there was something I could do about it. If I hurried home and ate quickly, I might still have time to dress and find a church somewhere. At least I could try!

Chapter Five

CONVERSION

"Go to church!" Beulah replied in astonishment at my pronouncement.

"Go to church and *get saved*, is what I said," I replied firmly.

"Then I want to go with you," she asserted.

I was both relieved and happy, for a change had already begun to take place within Beulah. For the last few weeks I had watched as she became soft and tender, and it was getting through to me. My already convicted spirit became even more aware of the heavy load I carried as I watched her read and pray. But even as I watched, I felt that I was not yet ready to make that change myself.

I had not made one comment to Beulah for fear that I would "upset the apple cart," so to say. I liked the change that I had seen in her and I wanted her to stay that way, but I was not certain that I wanted to follow her leading.

Now that I had come to the end, I, too, was ready for a regeneration process.

The transition in Beulah's life had come unexpectedly. A few short weeks ago, a crisis had happened. Her eldest brother, Jack, who was married and the father of two children, had been as physically fit and trim looking as in the high school days when he had played football and been selected for the Southwest Virginia All-Star team. Suddenly, he was lying in the hospital—on his death bed.

The powerful legs that had helped carry his team to victory now lay useless. He had been tackled by an opponent so small that it could be viewed only by a microscope.

"Poliomyelitis" was the doctor's grim verdict.

As Jack was lying in an iron lung, unable to even breathe on his own, Beulah was allowed a few minutes to visit with him. For hours he had been unconscious, but now as she softly spoke his name he began to respond, turning slowly and looking into her eyes.

"Beulah, honey, I love you," he said faintly as she leaned forward and strained to listen to the weak words he uttered.

No more words were spoken as he turned back to sleep, and tears filled Beulah's eyes.

The words "I love you" had cut through Beulah's heart like a knife for she had never remembered him or any of her brothers or sister ever expressing such tenderness.

The words continued to haunt her the rest of the night as she and the others kept their vigil, returning to our home the next morning to rest while still others took their shift.

After everyone went home to rest, Beulah also left. The next morning, she came over to the bottling plant and picked up the books. She wanted to work on them at home to be near the phone. But, as she attempted to work she found that she couldn't concentrate. She couldn't add or subtract. She couldn't even remember what two-plus-two was. Nothing made any sense to her.

All of a sudden she broke down in tears. She cried and cried, and shaking with sobs, she finally said, "Oh, God, if there is a God in heaven, hear me. If You'll spare my brother Jack and prove You are real, I'll serve You the rest of my life."

Just a few days later, she ended up in the hospital with a case of bursitis. The need for something to give her understanding and comfort in this experience caused her to ask our daughter Wanda to bring her a Bible.

She had not been raised in a religious atmosphere and knew nothing of how to reach God. But, our frustrations at home with the business, and with our family life, and now her brother's illness, had brought her to the place where she needed to reach out for something and the Bible was the only thing she could think of... the very thing which in her earlier life had been needless and neglected. Having nothing else to do but lie there, she finished it within a few days.

She returned home after an eight-day stay, only to continue to read and pray for her brother Jack's recovery.

This kind of surrender was a new experience to her. She had claimed that she was a Methodist, but it was only because she had attended a few times as a small child.

The only other time I could ever remember her calling on God was when, as a young mother giving birth to our first and only child, she had called on Him in a life and death struggle for her own life.

Following birth complications, heavy hemorraging had begun that the doctor could not arrest. The situation became so critical that she later remembered her spirit leaving her body and floating up to the ceiling where she had looked back at her still form lying on the bed.

Before unconsciousness had enveloped her, she, in her weak voice, had asked someone to get "Old Sister Maggard" to come and pray. Sister Maggard was the valley "fanatic." As a child Beulah had known her only as someone to be avoided because of her strange ways. On many occasions, she could be heard praying aloud as neighbors walked near her home. Many had testified to being healed from her prayers.

Now, as the doctor had put it, "Her life is as critical as the turning of a hand."

Beulah had cried out desperately for the only person she knew who could get a prayer answered.

As consciousness returned, Beulah turned to see the tear-stained face of Sister Maggard (who had put every one else out of the room); her hand was stroking Beulah's hair and she proclaimed assuredly, "You'll be all right now."

A soft piercing cry coming from the other room caused Beulah to raise her head up from her pillow and ask that our new daughter be brought in. Soon mother and daughter were united, and the satisfied sounds of a nursing infant greatly comforted Beulah.

Although aware that God had answered our prayers and spared my wife, the thought to serve God simply did not penetrate our self-centered way of life.

But now that this new peace had come upon her, Beulah began to realize God would give her brother his life, too. And when she went to the hospital to visit him a few days after her own dismissal, she found that the doctors had a different prognosis. Jack's condition had changed... he was improving. He would live!

Beulah took to the Word of God like a new duckling takes to water. She plunged in enthusiastically. Her appetite for spiritual truths caused her to eagerly devour the words of each sacred page. She began to read day and night. I left the house to go to work in the morning and she would be curled up in bed reading. I came home at noon expecting lunch, and finding that nothing had been prepared for she would be on the couch reading.

In the evening, it was often the same. But I was afraid to say anything because she spoke softly and had such a pleasant attitude. I was afraid if I complained, something would change. I realized she had received salvation, and I became convicted of my own attitude in thinking that I could do without God.

Now this particular night had finally brought me to the point where I *must* make a decision to change.

I went on talking in an emotional effort to explain. "Beulah, honey, I've gotta do *something*. I've been so miserable the last few years and to make it even worse, your reading and praying has me under greater conviction. I can't even wait until Sunday. I've got to get saved tonight!" I was emphatic and on the verge of tears.

We both rushed upstairs and dressed hurriedly for church. I was glad that she was going with me, for although a change had come over her and created within her a new nature, she had not yet attended a church service.

"This can't be," I proclaimed agitatedly to Beulah. "You mean they're not having church service here tonight either?"

This was the third church we had found that Saturday evening with the lights off and not a soul to be found.

"But I thought everyone had church on Saturday night," I mused aloud, remembering back to my earlier life when Saturday services were on the regular agenda.

"Well, I just know that this little church down the road is having service tonight." So we soon found ourselves out on the road leading to the little country church where indeed a service was already well under way.

Taking a seat toward the rear, I drank in every word of every song, testimony and sermon that was uttered that night. I soaked it up like a thirsty sponge.

When the invitation was given, I decided to go forward and give my heart and life to God. I was about to burst apart at the seams from my pent-up emotions. But before I could step out into the aisle another young man closer to the front broke into a sob and rushed forward to kneel at the front. Soon he was joined by two men (I assumed that they were deacons) who each took him by an arm and raised him to his feet where the pastor stood waiting to shake his hand and accept his confession of faith. From my seat I watched as on three occasions the man attempted in vain to kneel down and pray in the fashion I had been accustomed to. It didn't take me long to realize that a display of emotionalism was distasteful to the members of this congregation.

I just couldn't go down there, for I needed somewhere that I could bawl and squawl out to the Lord. I determined in my heart that I would have to find a church where I could kneel down before an old-fashioned mourner's bench until I knew God had heard me and that my sins had been forgiven.

About this time an elderly lady had made her way back to the bench where we now stood and asked, "Young man, are you saved?"

Not wanting to lie, I quickly recalled that Dad had preached you were saved by grace through faith and acceptance of Jesus Christ, and fearing humilation if I went forward there (for I would surely overflow with tears), I determined in my heart at that moment that I was going to live for God. I turned to the woman and replied, "By God's grace, *I am saved.*"

"Like a blue-tick hound on the trail of a raccoon," the next evening found me again on the trail in search of God. Soon we found a church where the lights shone brightly through the windows and joyful singing penetrated the walls and the cool December breeze wafted the melody clear out into the parking lot and into my chest.

Once again I drank in the Word of God as it was sung and preached. When the altar call was given, I rushed forward under great conviction to the altar, with the anticipation that sin's burden of guilt would soon be lifted. As I began to sob and pray and pray and sob, joy and peace soon replaced the guilt and emptiness.

As we walked out into the cold December night, and I looked up . . . how long it had been since I had looked up!! . . . I looked into God's big heaven, and realized the vastness of His universe and the miracle that He had taken notice of *me*. Again, thankfulness swelled in and filled my heart.

Right away, I began to notice a change in our lives. We now worked together with little strain between us. We studied God's Word diligently. I realized also that a miracle had taken place in my body, for upon receiving salvation God had healed me of my heart condition, and also of ulcers and hemorrhoids.

We began to tell others of our conversion. I felt that I had to call my mother. Upon receiving the phone call, she didn't hesitate, but caught a plane the very next day and flew to Kingsport, Tennessee. Arriving at the airport, the first words she uttered were, "Clifton, is it really true? I had to come and see for myself."

We embraced jubilantly and returned home, with Beulah and I competing for my mother's attention, each of us trying to express ourselves first.

Mother was overwhelmed by the volume of words which broke forth in a torrent. There was such joy that evening it seemed that nothing could break the harmony until Mom asked us, "Have you both been baptized in water yet?"

"We plan to be just as soon as we can," I replied.

"I don't feel baptism in water is necessary," Beulah stated matter-of-factly.

"I guess that was the way she was raised to think about baptism," I thought to myself.

No amount of persuasion from Mom and I could change her resistance to what we felt was the second important step of faith in following the commandment of the Lord. It took a revelation from the Lord to convince her that her way of thinking was out of harmony with the Scriptures. When that happened, we decided we wanted to be baptized that very weekend.

We had not yet affiliated ourselves with any church, and a friend of ours, whom we were visiting with that day, arranged for his pastor to baptize us. He eagerly consented to do so, even though it was on Christmas Day.

There, with only my mother-in-law and two friends to witness, we followed the example of the Lord and were baptized by immersion in a little church in Big Stone Gap, Virginia.

Chapter Six

SLAVERY

If I thought salvation automatically solved every problem, like the last page of a novel where everyone lives happily ever after, I was soon brought back to reality.

Although the Spirit of God was now a new element in my life, and I knew what it meant to be a new creature in Christ Jesus, one of the old things that hadn't passed away was my craving for cigarettes.

For the first few days after my conversion smoking hadn't provoked any conviction. But I became so zealous to tell others about Jesus, that I would witness to anyone, anywhere. Then I began to notice that as I talked their eyes would inadvertantly be drawn to my left shirt pocket which bulged, revealing the outline of a package of cigarettes. I knew then that they were a hindrance to an effective testimony and that I had to get rid of them.

On New Year's Day, 1957, I resolved to myself, "I will quit smoking these things."

Our search for a church home led us to a full-gospel church where we were warmly received. Upon leaving the services that evening, the pastor spoke to me and said, "Brother and Sister Snodgrass, we trust you enjoyed our service. We welcome you to become a part of our congregation."

I replied, "I would like to very much, but I feel that I should confess that I do smoke."

Even at that moment I wanted to get outside so I could satisfy the hunger that had gnawed inside since early in the service.

He asked understandingly, "Would you like me to pray for you?"

Now I did not really want him to pray for me, I wanted to hurry outside to smoke. But feeling that courtesy demanded an affirmative answer, I shook my head yes.

He then laid his hand on my head and began to pray that God would deliver me.

The craving for another cigarette was unabated following that prayer, but I decided that I was man enough to whip the habit on my own. I drove home determined not to smoke that evening.

I did fairly well that night, but by ten o'clock the next morning it was really getting to me. I had intended to show the devil that I was a bigger man than he was, but I soon learned that I was wrong.

Up until this time, I had not taken the cigarettes from my pocket, just to prove I could be around them and not be tempted. I walked out of the bottling plant to our home next door, and mounted the stairs to be alone in the privacy of the bathroom. I decided there, "I'll just have to smoke one."

I pulled the cigarettes from my pocket, and nervously took one out. I placed it between my lips and drew out my lighter. Just as I raised my hands to light it, I suddenly realized what I was doing and began to talk to myself. "Now you've gone this far. Don't ruin it now."

I took the cigarette from my lips and returned it to the pack. As I did, something overcame me that was more powerful than my own will—I called it a nicotine spirit. It took hold of me and my mind lost all its reason. It didn't take long to get a cigarette out of the pack and put it in my mouth again and light it up.

I took my first long draw. "Ahhh...," I thought, "now maybe I'll calm down a little." Then a sensation that I had never felt before registered in my stomach. Something started churning around inside like fire and came up into my throat and nasal passages. I felt it all over my face.

"What's going on here?" I questioned aloud. Panicky thoughts raced through my brain. Quickly I stood and looked into the mirror. I wasn't prepared for what I saw. It looked like my own face, but yet it wasn't my face. A terrifying image seemed to superimpose itself over my reflection. The most incredible feature was my eyes. They seemed to be shooting out streaks of fire. Fear shot through my entire body. I thought I was looking at old Lucifer himself. "I must be going crazy," I thought as I pushed my way out the door and made a mad scramble down the stairs.

"Beulah . . . Beulah. Come here, quick! Where are you?" I yelled at the top of my voice. I grew even more panicky when I thought she was slow in responding.

She came around the corner from the kitchen and met me head on.

"What's wrong, Cliff? What's the matter with you? You just about scared me to death!"

I grabbed her and made her look me straight in the face.

"Beulah, honey, look at me. What do you see?" I asked pleadingly.

"I don't see anything," was all she could answer.

"Well, now, look close. Look in my eyes, don't you see fire in them?"

"I don't see anything," she repeated. "What are you so excited about?"

I couldn't take time to answer her. I had to see again for myself and even though I was afraid to look, my curiosity overcame my fear. I took the stairs two at a time, rushed back into the bathroom and pushed my face to within two inches of mirror. There it was. I could still see the fire. I sat down dazed and bewildered.

"That's it!" I said to myself with new determination. "That's is it!" I knew in that second, that minute, that I would never again touch another cigarette as long as I lived.

"I'll die first," I renewed my determination over again.

However, after that fear left me, the struggle to keep that vow was not easy.

My battle with the smoking habit caused many sleepless nights in the days following. The third and fourth night found me walking the lonely streets. God had not taken the habit from me, but had given me a will to overcome it. As I walked those dark streets lit here and there by an occasional lamppost, I talked to Him. And here and there His light touched me and brought me out of darkness and the bondage of that habit. My determination grew as did my understanding. Because of this particular manner of deliverance, God has given me compassion for those who are slaves to similiar habits.

I have come in contact with those who need that compassion, and through prayer, I have been used to cast the nicotine spirit out of them. I could minister to them because I understood what it was like to be a slave myself.

Chapter Seven

ON THE WINGS OF A DOVE

As I continued to hear and study God's Word, and began to receive understanding, the realization that I lacked something in my spiritual life began to grow. I noted that the men in the New Testament really had power from God and I knew that I didn't. And most of the sermons I heard seemed to centralize on the theme of the baptism of the Holy Ghost (Holy Spirit). As I mused over this, my mind reflected back to all those miracles I had seen manifested in the saints when I was a child at home and I remembered hearing my father preach, "Have ye received the Holy Ghost since ye believed?" I jumped to my feet in the sudden realization that what I needed was indeed this baptism in the Holy Spirit which gave power to the believers. I purposed then and there in my heart that I must and would have this baptism.

"I'm going to have it," I determined. "I'll be the first one to the altar and the last to leave. I'll be the first one to testify every opportunity given, too."

My hunger for the Lord made attending church a joy. I was there almost every night. When the invitation was given for those who wanted to draw closer to God, I was seldom second in kneeling at the altar.

I began to attend revival services in every full-gospel church in town whenever there wasn't one in my own church. Each time the pastor or evangelist concluded the service with, "Now, who wants to receive the Holy Ghost tonight?" my hand would be the first to go up.

Yet, although I boldly proclaimed that I wanted the baptism in the Holy Ghost, I was not as bold in praying for it. I would kneel down at the altar and begin to whisper my supplication to God. I heard others around me praying loudly and fervently and I thought, "Oh, I wish I could be that bold, but I don't know how to pray."

Timidity would then take hold of me and with that the devil would move in on the scene and whisper in my ear, "Everyone can hear what you're saying."

I couldn't seem to overcome that fear. It haunted me. But, I continued to go forward and pray meekly, "God, give me the Holy Ghost."

Finally, one night I found a place where the voices of three good brethren who were praying around me grew so loud that they drowned out the voice of the devil. I thought to myself, "This is heaven."

I boldly praised God at that little church in Kingsport, Tennessee, and those brethren stayed right with me as long as I prayed. Whenever I moved, no matter what direction, forward, backward, shifting from side to side from fatigue, they moved also. They stayed about the same distance from me, one on each side and one in front. I was encouraged to "Seek the Lord, brother, until you're satisfied."

Finally after about an hour passed, I was completely exhausted. My face was wet with perspiration and my voice was only a hoarse whisper. My heart felt so full and still I was unsatisfied. I closed my eyes, and the tears that had welled up were pushed out and ran freely down my cheeks. The pain of despair was so great that I began to shake with sobs. I had been so confident that I would receive that night. "Oh, God," I cried, "I don't know what else to do. Lord, I'm worn out now, thirsty for the Holy Ghost. I've done everything I know to do."

Disappointed, I rose to return to my seat. Going down the aisle, I felt a hand on my shoulder and turned to see who touched me. The old grey-haired evangelist who had preached that night stood facing me.

His touch did something to me. I felt a tingling run all through me as I became aware of the presence and power of God.

He looked deep into my eyes and spoke prophetically. "God told me to tell you that He has a gift for you that will cause you to find favor with men."

I had no idea what he was talking about and not wanting to be rude, I simply said, "Thank you."

But as I proceeded to the back, I felt God's glory come down and rest upon me. I didn't feel like running, jumping or shouting, but instead a peace settled upon me as if I were encased inside a big tunnel that seemed to reach all the way to heaven. I had never sensed anything like this before, but nevertheless, I knew somehow, that it was the spirit of the Lord resting upon me, and I didn't want to come out of it.

At first, I wondered what Beulah was going to say about what she had seen and heard. To my surprise, she never said a word to me, but seemed to stare in amazement. She arose and followed me out to the company truck, which I had driven to church that evening, in complete silence.

The experience that followed was one I will never forget. I was surrounded by this aura of ecstasy. I was unaware of the trip home, when I started the engine, changed the gears, and made the turns. Beulah sat wordlessly on the other side. I could feel the force around me, a force which I felt would allow no danger to come near me. I drove home in God's big tunnel.

We had gone several blocks when I realized that Beulah was sitting as close to the opposite door as she could. Usually she sat in the middle of the seat and put her arm around me as I drove.

"I should ask her what's wrong," I thought to myself. But then I realized that I didn't really care. I knew that at this moment all I cared about was what was happening to me, for it was like nothing I had ever felt before. I drove that next three miles home under the influence of the Spirit of God, for I remember nothing of the drive, only the feeling of being at perfect peace with myself. As I pulled to a stop and parked in front of the house, Beulah slid out of the seat and ran up the steps. I didn't want to move. I felt perfectly content and was afraid this great emotion within my chest would leave if I had to move from its tranquility and take up the normal routine of life. But I knew I could not sit there in that truck all night; besides, Beulah was waiting for me to unlock the door.

I reached the porch and without saying a word, again unusual, she stepped aside for me to unlock the door.

I moved as if in a dream world, yet knowing

that what was happening was more real than what I had felt for years. I desired to do nothing but to get to bed quickly so that I could lay everything aside except my thoughts of this strange event.

We usually had a snack after church, but again my wife seemed as remote from me as another world, and what puzzled me even more was the fact that she was not questioning my strange behavior. On the contrary, it seemed as if she were avoiding me, which at the time suited me fine, for I couldn't have explained what was happening had she asked me.

I retired to bed immediately. Reaching over to set the alarm, I noticed the time was just ten o'clock. I had hardly stretched out in place and pulled the covers over me, when the most unusual thing happened; an experience that has never left me in all the years since.

"I was in the Spirit and it was the Lord's Day." The heavens opened up. The roof rolled back. No longer was it night, but perfect day.

The clouds were bright over my head. My eyes searched the sky, and suddenly I sighted, about a quarter of a mile up, a small circling object.

Sensing the importance of this event, my body strained to see what the speck was, not realizing that I had passed into "another" world of vision. Then I saw it. A small white dove.

As I watched, it made a dive right for my face like a dive bomber. I could not move, I only shook and trembled from top to bottom, bone and muscle. Then suddenly, within inches of my face, it turned and passed and swooped back into the heavens. As He passed by, it seemed as if warm water, like a tropical rain, was being poured into me, filling me even fuller than I was at church. My heart felt as if it could not hold another cupful of emotion. My love for God could never have been more perfect, but I did not know what to do with it.

I lay there and watched the little dove climb back up into the heavens again. As I watched Him circle around and around, I suddenly realized that He represented the Holy Ghost. Then I saw He was preparing to make another dive toward me again. This time He passed within inches of my face and was so close I could feel the flutter of His wings as He passed by. Again He reascended. He did not tarry as long this time, but made several more trips, swooping down and each time coming lower and closer to my face. And each time it seemed as if a shock wave of glorious power would pass through my body. Every fibre of my being, even the marrow of my bones seemed to be drenched with this power.

Finally I began to reason to myself. "The next time that dove passes by my face, I'll stick out my tongue. If my tongue can just touch even the tip of His wings, I believe I will receive the baptism of the Holy Ghost."

Reaching out with my tongue seemed logical to me for I was totally incapable of moving the rest of my limbs. I was so overcome by this glorious power that they were as dead weights to me.

No sooner had the thought passed, when the dove began its power dive toward me again. As He came closer, I made every effort to stick my tongue straight out of my mouth as far as I could reach. To my amazement, it seemed that I had lost control over it also. I was like a drunken man, intoxicated with the Spirit. I could not control my muscles at all and found that my tongue, instead of standing straight out, fell uselessly into the lower corner of my mouth.

I had just been saying, "Halleulah! Praise you, Jesus!" but now it seemed that I was hearing myself speak another language.

My satisfaction was complete. I was enveloped in this wonderful power. Again and again, as I vainly tried this strange method to reach the dove, my tongue would fall this way and that and perform those wonderful words of praise to the Savior.

Perhaps an hour or two passed and then the Lord's Spirit began to speak to my spirit.

"Your wife has a headache. I want to prove

to you that what you are experiencing is real. Touch her with your hand and I'll heal her of that headache."

Immediately I responded, "But, Lord, You don't know my wife like I do. She's funny about things like that. Give me a few minutes to think this over." I lay there in that bed, not even aware that God surely knew my wife better than I. After all, all this was still quite new to me. I pondered, "How am I going to be able to do what the Lord told me?"

But knowing that I had promised to do everything God asked, I lay there considering how I could lay my hands on Beulah without causing her to get upset with me.

Then I decided, "I'll move my hand slowly and just barely touch her and maybe she'll never know it."

I took my left hand then and slowly slid it up to my chest and as silently as possible glided it across my body and over the pillow until I felt her hair. Then extending just my fingertips, I stretched them until they lightly touched her forehead. As I made contact with her skin I felt a power shoot out through my hand.

As I moved back into position, I came out of the Spirit and into my natural senses. I turned over, elated at the experience I had just been through. God had seen my hunger; He knew my longing. Not until after the vision did I realize that what had happened was according to the Scriptures. As John the Baptist had seen the Dove of the Holy Spirit descend upon Jesus, even now my eyes had beheld the speck moving toward me—a pure white dove. I looked at the clock. It was one o'clock in the morning. I had been in the Spirit for about three hours!

The next morning I decided to tell Beulah about it. I felt I would burst open at the seams if I didn't tell someone. When I got to the part about touching her, she had her own story to tell.

She knew that something was happening even in the previous evening service. As I had risen from prayer and moved back to where she sat waiting, she felt a sanctifying power extend from my body to hers. Not having ever felt anything like this, it had left her speechless while she savored the experience.

She had been awake during my whole vision, knowing that something beyond her understanding was going on. The instant that I touched her that night she was aware of a strange power that flowed through her, and the headache, which she had indeed had, fled immediately.

I wasn't quite sure what to do with the experience that had visited me. It seemed that no one had ever seen anything like it. I listened to everyone else's testimony of how they received the gift of the baptism of the

Holy Ghost and comparing mine with theirs, I became unsure of myself.

"Surely," I thought to myself, "you have to have a bolt of lightning strike you or see a ball of fire or pass out."

With these doubts occupying my thoughts, the assurance that I had was replaced by uncertainty. As a result, I didn't manifest the baptism in the Holy Ghost for nearly a year, and it cost me many hours of exhausting and needless tarrying.

Chapter Eight

THE BARRIER

Bankruptcy? Impossible! Yet as I lay in my bed that morning reviewing the most recent account of my business ledgers, bankruptcy seemed to be the only solution to my pressing financial dilemma. The figures in the debit column had emblazened themselves upon my mind. As I closed my eyes, the red numbers vividly announced their dreaded message like a neon sign advertising a place of business.

It was Saturday morning and I was all alone. I had tossed in restless sleep through the long night. The longer I lay there the greater the weight grew in my troubled heart.

I was facing the end, the lonely end. In fact, there was no one left in the house but my daughter's cocker spaniel, Taffy. It wasn't just my finances that were in difficulty, but also my family crisis was at its peak.

My wife had left me to go to her mother's for

a visit. The very atmosphere of the house had become one of continual tension. My daughter had been in a state of rebellion and declared that she would no longer live with us. She had just completed her graduation and true to her words had left for Dayton, Ohio.

But not only was I alone physically, I was alone spiritually. My amazing spiritual experience with the dove seemed remote now. I certainly did not feel the joyful elation that I had the night of my vision. And, my lack of joy caused a lack of faith, which in turn produced a lack of confidence and a great deal of tension. This, in itself, caused the emotional crisis which prevented Beulah from receiving the pentecostal experience in her own life, and resulted in her escape to Big Stone for a while to get away from the pressure. My loneliness and frustration had reached the heights. As I lay there with only the whimpering comfort of the small dog trying to nuzzle close to me, mingled emotions pressed upon me.

What was I to do? Surely there was a solution for my dilemma. "Oh, God," my heart cried out, "what am I going to do?"

While lying there, I thought back over the last few years. Had all this happened in so short a time? Just a few years ago, it seemed that financially I had all that I had ever needed. When I bought this business, I had expected to make even more.

I remembered my brother-in-law's comment, "Looks like you'll make a killing." But instead of making a killing, the finances were killing me. From January to August, I had received only nine hundred dollars income for myself. Right at this moment I had eight families to pay and no money to pay them with. I couldn't even afford to pay my eighty dollars salary to myself. I had thirteen hundred dollars worth of uncashable checks stuck in the china cupboard drawer.

Now I had to get up and face the day and reveal to those eight men on my payroll that the following Monday morning there would be no work, for I had no money for flavoring syrup or sugar to begin preparation for bottling the pop.

I began to weep and cry. A strong desire for the Lord's direction descended upon me. I had been trying to sell the plant and I had had a tentative buyer, but when he went over my books and found it was a losing proposition he called it all off.

I knew that the Lord was my only source of hope. I slid out of the bed and down on my knees.

"Oh, God," I cried out. "I need Your help, Lord, I don't have the money to pay the men today. I don't have the money to buy supplies to make the soft drinks, or for gas for the trucks, much less the repair work that needs to be done on them. There's no money to support my family or pay the bills. Lord, I can't even pay my tithes. It isn't as if I don't want to. Lord, You know I'm honest; I plan to pay just as soon as I get ahead. I've been keeping record. See, Lord, I've got it recorded in this little book here. I know exactly how much I owe You, thirty-six dollars and twenty-one cents, but right now I can't even cash my checks for myself."

Then I began to cry. I prayed as loud as I could. I wanted to make sure God heard me. I cried until I was limp and exhausted. Even the poor little dog seemed to sense my sorrow. I felt her rough little tongue licking my hand as if in some way she wanted to let me know she felt my loneliness; she whimpered in sympathy.

Then, just at the moment when I felt I couldn't say another word or cry another tear, I heard that Voice.

"Son, could you go to the grocery store and buy food if you hadn't paid the bill?"

"No, Sir," I replied.

"Could you cash a check at the bank if you didn't have any money deposited there?"

"No, Lord," I replied earnestly.

"Well, what would happen, son?" the Voice gently pressed for an answer.

"Well, Lord, if I wrote a check, it would bounce, of course. Lord, you know that."

Then imploringly, "Well, son, it works the same way in spiritual things. You must put the things of God first. If you don't deposit anything in the bank of heaven, how do you expect to draw from its reserves?"

Understanding flashed as lightning across the darkened sky of my mind.

I jumped up quickly and dressed, my mind racing impatiently with preparation for what I was about to do. I hurried downstairs and got out all the checks that were in the drawer. I picked out the smallest one, fifty dollars, reasoning to myself that it took six days to get the check cleared and perhaps by then I could accumulate enough money for a deposit. Putting the check in my shirt pocket, I hastened across the street to the bank and cashed it. Placing the money in my billfold as I left the bank, I began to contemplate where I was going to pay this tithe money to the Lord. Beulah and I had only been attending church for a few months now; each weekend at a different location. As yet, we had made no firm decision on which church we intended to join. But at this point I really didn't care where the money went, I was just happy to settle my account with the Lord. And I did not intend to run up a bill with Him again, ever! I had received a new understanding of the relationship that I, as a new child, should have with his Father.

I crossed the street, intending to go back to the bottling plant and see if I could catch up on some of the work that was waiting for me.

I had scarcely arrived when I heard a car

pull up and the door slam shut. I looked out to see Reverend Bobby Sams, pastor of a new church near Kingsport, approaching the entrance, making his weekly visit.

Brother Sams pastored a small, struggling congregation which barely paid ten dollars a week. With four small children, the luxury of soft drinks was to him like buying tickets for the opera. So, each Saturday morning Brother Sams would bring an empty case of pop bottles and I would give him a full case of mixed soft drinks in return.

We exchanged brief Christian greetings with a comment on the weather. An inspiration suddenly came to me that here was a man of God who certainly needed tithe money. I made up my mind right then to give him half of it.

"Brother Sams," I interjected, "I have some tithes I owe the Lord. Here is twenty dollars."

"Praise the Lord!" he exclaimed raising his hands and dancing for joy right there in the street.

"Brother Snodgrass, I just got off my knees not more than twenty minutes ago. I prayed, 'Lord, I need forty dollars and I don't know where I'm going to get it. No one owes me anything and none of my members can afford to give it to me.' I was trying to fix up a few bicycles to sell, but, praise the Lord, here's half of it!"

I was so thrilled by his enthusiasm, I

reached into my shirt pocket, pulled out another twenty dollars and thrust it into Brother Sams hand.

"Then here's the other half of it," I said half-laughing and half-crying.

You should have seen Brother Bobby then as he danced, shouted, and cried all at the same time. It didn't even matter to him who saw him.

He went on his way rejoicing and soon I was alone once again. The ringing of the phone brought me back to reality with its still pressing worries.

"Mr. Snodgrass," the voice on the phone began, "I have done a lot of thinking. I know that there are risks, but I have decided to buy your bottling plant anyway."

I could hardly contain my voice to talk in an accepted businesslike tone. Soon, however, all details for the transaction were worked out.

Dazedly, I returned the phone to its cradle. Scarcely a half-hour had passed since I knelt in prayer seeking for the key to a seemingly locked door. But instead of a key-lock, it was a combination lock. The combination of prayer, obedience and faith had opened the lock and I was soon on the victorious side.

Chapter Nine

NEW BEGINNING

It was with a great sense of relief I placed my copy of the sales contract of the bottling plant in my personal business file. The money from the sale of the business had been devoured by my creditors, yet I still had the feeling of waking up from a nightmare. I almost felt like pinching myself to see if it were true that the ordeal was finally over.

Soon, I was on my way back to Dayton, Ohio, where I hoped to make a fresh start.

I arrived alone, broke, and wounded in my pride.

Beulah had left again for a visit to the home of her parents in Big Stone Gap, Virginia, awaiting my decision for our future. There, cloaking herself in the comfortable surroundings of her hometown, she began the task of establishing a home. It was her desire that we make our home there where I had once been a business partner with my father-in-law and my brother-in-law in the Powell Furniture Company. Beulah was so hopeful that this is where we should be that she had donned working clothes and a nail-apron and actually started building a house on a lot which we had purchased years earlier.

Uncertain of exactly the right move to make, I arrived in Dayton, where Wanda had been staying since graduation.

For the next few weeks, I was totally dependent on my daughter for my financial needs as she paid the rent, bought the groceries and paid the bills. When I needed spending money, my brother-in-law, Dude Owens, insisted upon pressing a ten or twenty dollar bill in my hand. I ate humble pie for the remainder.

The employment picture in Dayton was bleak.

"I'm sorry, we don't have any jobs available," was a very familiar statement.

"If we have anything available, we'll call you." How many times did I hear those words?

This was really a trying time. I had prayed and earnestly entreated the Lord, but the end was not in sight.

Oh, I was still blessed spiritually. I had found a group of believers at the nearby Evangelism Center where I had found warm fellowship and spiritual enrichment as I feasted on the Word.

I longed to share with Wanda, but she was bent upon her own way, feeling that she was old enough to be on her own. And what could I say with her supporting me? We had no spiritual fellowship for she refused to think of Jesus Christ, she was too busy planning her own future.

Though the trials were severe and I was lonely, I never once entertained the notion of giving up on God. In fact, serving Him was still uppermost in my mind.

When I was offered a job delivering alcoholic beverages to grocery stores and taverns I refused, even though the wages were attractive.

"I hate to prolong my dependency upon you. I know it doesn't leave you with much, but I just don't think the Lord would be pleased for me to carry beer and wine into places where a Christian shouldn't go," I told Wanda that evening.

"But, Dad, you used to drive a beer truck," she replied.

"Yes, honey, before World War II, I used to make a weekly run from Big Stone Gap to Chicago where I would get a load to bring back to a local distributor. But, I'm saved now and I'm afraid I just couldn't do it."

I was becoming really concerned about my

job situation. It looked bleak. I encouraged myself daily with, "It'll be better tomorrow. Something will turn up. The Lord is faithful."

All I could see was the problem of finding a job, but I kept forgetting God doesn't have *problems*, He has *plans*.

When it rains, it pours, and this was a good rain. After turning down the beverage truck route on Friday, I was overwhelmed the following day as five jobs became available at once.

Careful consideration was given to selecting the right one. I didn't want a job which would require my working Sundays because I wanted to give that day to the Lord. Each job had its drawbacks. I finally decided to take the route salesman position for the Blue Bird Pie Company. The only drawback to that job was the long hours and low pay. But, the pie company had decided to hire me even though there were no established routes open.

"Because of your previous experience, Mr. Snodgrass," the supervisor informed me, "we will give you a truck, load it with pies, head you toward Muncie, Indiana, and you are on your own to establish a route."

Once again I was an employee. It had been two years since I had been told to get a supervisor's job. My efforts to be an employer had ended in disaster, but now I had an opportunity to climb out of the financial hole I had fallen into.

The Blue Bird Pie truck with its delicious aroma of freshly baked pies soon became a sanctuary where I fellowshipped with God daily as I drove the 180 miles of my route, servicing over seventy stops at restaurants and grocery stores along the way.

And hearing of my new job, Beulah abandoned her building project in Virginia and soon we were a happy family again. Did I say happy? Anyway, we were together again. Wanda still kept her distance from Beulah and watched us both. She was still suspicious of Beulah's new behavior, as her mother seemed to spare no effort to show concern and consideration.

The little extra treats in her lunch along with an occasional note only added to Wanda's confusion about the change.

I was delighted with the new Beulah.

Many times, even before entering the door of our home after work, I would receive a witness of the Holy Spirit that assured me that Beulah had been praying and searching her Bible that day.

Thus, we grew closer and began to pray together that Wanda would soon be united with us in Christian fellowship.

Chapter Ten

NIGHT VISITOR

We attended church every night at every opportunity. One time we attended a thirty-day revival and didn't miss a single night. Considering the hours I had to work—5 A.M. until about 5 in the afternoon—this was quite a sacrifice for me. I came to the place several times during that revival where I had to ask several men of the church to lay hands on me for the strength to work the next day.

Every night I prayed for the Holy Ghost, still not having enough faith to believe that my former experience, the visit of the little "dove," was the way it should happen.

When I thought about it a big lump rose up in my throat, tears would come to my eyes, and my heart would ache, because no one seemed to be able to tell me what to do to turn loose this reservoir of God's power that had collected inside me and needed to flow out.

During this revival, the evangelist asked, "Who wants to receive the Holy Ghost?"

(I was still sticking my hand up in the air first for anything God had on the menu.)

The evangelist saw my arm go up and with a beckoning hand questioned, "Would you come up here?"

"Sure," I replied out loud, hoping with all my heart that this was the night for me. Anticipation grew as I mounted the platform. He had me stand with my face towards the audience and he held the microphone near my mouth.

He then proceeded to take hold of my adam's apple and shake it up and down. He prayed while doing so, and then commanded me, "Now speak in tongues."

But I did not speak in tongues. In my fear of the Lord I was cautious, not wanting to do anything that wasn't definitely of God. Besides, I'd never heard of anyone getting the baptism of the Holy Ghost in this way before!

Again a few nights later, the pastor of the church asked, "Who wants the Holy Ghost tonight?"

My hand shot up without hesitation. The pastor looked in my direction and seemed to sigh. I knew he was becoming provoked with me.

Every night I had been in that prayer line along with my sister and my wife. They, too, were now seeking for God to fill them with His Holy Spirit.

The prayer line moved forward with many of the people ahead of me receiving a healing or a blessing. My expectation grew.

I was next. I walked up to stand in front of the pastor and others who were helping him pray.

He gripped me firmly on the shoulder and said, "Now you repeat after me and you'll get the Holy Ghost. Eli, eli, lama sabachthani, say that."

I asserted firmly, somewhat shocked, "No, I'm not going to say that."

"Why?" he sighed.

"Why, that's what Jesus said when He was dying on the cross. I don't want God to forsake me."

The pastor got very disgusted, let go of me and moved to the next person in line while I walked away with a deflated feeling.

Still, as that revival neared its completion, I continued my quest for an infilling.

Several nights later, we were all standing around in the after-service seeking God. I began to ask Him again to fill me with the Holy Ghost.

While I was praying for a downpour of the "latter rain," it began to really rain outside.

A strong wind came up and as the building was only partially finished, there were several leaky places where the wind began to blow the rain in. I happened to be standing in one of those places.

With an upturned face and raised hands, I had been praising God and praying sincerely for the Spirit for almost an hour when the rain began to drip through the ceiling and hit my face. But I was feeling the presence of the Lord and without someone to tell me it would be okay to move, I stood my ground. I was afraid if I made even a step I would lose the touch of God I was now feeling, and I was so hungry for His presence, that I just stood there and let it rain in my face and down onto my clothes.

I really became hungry for God during that revival. It had been about a year since I had unknowingly received the baptism in the Holy Spirit through the vision, but all my faith seemed to have come to a standstill. I could not accept it because of my narrow thinking. I had my mind made up that I would still see a ball of fire, or be knocked down on the floor, or swoon. Since I hadn't done any of these things, I still refused to accept the experience that I had received back in Kingsport.

Then, one day on my way to Muncie, Indiana, for my daily pie route, I began to think again about what I could do to receive.

"Lord, I must have the baptism in the Holy Spirit, for I don't know where I stand with you. Help me!"

I began confessing all my faults to Him. Although I knew God's power was upon my life; still, as far as I knew *then,* I had not spoken in tongues.

I agonized for the sheer hunger I felt for this ability. Suddenly, an idea took hold of me as I talked to God. "Now, Lord, this is Tuesday morning. If you will allow me breakfast and black coffee, so that I can have the strength to work and drive these one hundred-ninety miles each day, I promise You, I will not eat extra breakfast, and I will fast the two other meals the rest of this week."

Although there was no audible voice, I felt as I waited on an answer from the Lord, that this would be permissible. It would mean a five-day fast.

By Saturday, I was really weak, working hard all day and faithfully attending each remaining night of the revival. Expectancy coupled with anxiety filled me as I entered church the last night of my fast.

I had arrived early so that I could go to the prayer room, which was upstairs, for a while before the service began.

Several of the brothers were already there and upon hearing my earnest prayers soon gathered around me, praying with me and laying their hands on my forehead, asking God to fill me this night.

The power of God overwhelmed me with

such a jolt that it felt as if someone's big fist had hit me in the forehead and knocked me across the room.

I staggered at the recoil of that power-punch and fell onto a cane chair with a post on the corner of the seat. Some worried that I had hurt myself, but as my head hit, I felt as if a big pillow or cushion had been placed under it.

I struggled to get up, while those men pressed me back, suggesting, "Why don't you just lie still there, brother, and relax and let the Lord fill you there. You'll be more comfortable."

"Oh, no," I answered. "It felt so good, I want to get up and get knocked down again."

I got up only to begin dancing in the Spirit. It took no effort of my own; in fact, it was as if I was having a tough time just touching my feet to the floor. Service was in progress by now downstairs, and all the congregation could do was sing for all the commotion and clamor I was making upstairs. They couldn't conduct any other part of the service.

Yet, even with that heavy anointing upon me, my mouth seemed to have a bridle on it which refused to be removed to let one word escape that was motivated by the Spirit.

Finally, we descended the stairs to the auditorium. As I entered, many people stared at the glow that radiated from my face.

Later that night, while I tossed and turned

in bed, still dwelling upon the service that had ended just a few hours ago, my wife lay in blissful sleep. It had been exhilarating and I had expectantly felt that I would achieve my one purpose—be filled with the Spirit. But it had not taken place that I could see.

I began to moan and blubber as the flood of tears broke loose and I gave vent to my profound passion.

I appealed to the Lord, "Oh, Lord, I have wasted a whole week. I have prayed and fasted and still I have not received the Holy Ghost."

I felt crushed and inconsolable. I bawled and boohooed and the Lord heard me.

I turned my eyes to look toward the doorway of our bedroom. As I did, the Lord unclogged my spiritual eyes and they were accessible to the Spirit-world.

I saw Him! JESUS!

He had on under garments, that I could see, which shone through the outer garment He wore. The outer one was a coat that hung just below His knees. It seemed as if all of His clothing consisted of the same material. Every thread sparkled whiter than the whitest white. In this vision, I could see the size of His body through His clothing. He was about five feet, ten or eleven inches tall and appeared to weigh about one hundred and ninety pounds. His hair was neat and clean and fell just above His collar. He had His back towards me. One arm rested upon the door casing and the other rested at His side.

Without turning around, He spoke to me audibly, "Is this worth it?"

"Oh, yes, Lord," I cried with joy, "it is worth it." I was wide awake. I reached over to shake Beulah so that she could see Him, too. But He was gone by the time I aroused her and then I knew it was in His plan for only my eyes to view Him at that time.

Chapter Eleven

SHANDAH!

How thrilling to be driving the car and listening to such glorious singing as this, for surely its origin had to be from heaven! The trio, lifting their voices in perfect harmony all in an unknown language were . . . wonder of wonders . . . my wife, my sister and my daughter. It was beyond description.

"God, I can never thank You enough for the *past* blessings You have poured out upon me, but this is even better!" I thought as I drove home from that service.

Yes, God had reunited my family, not just physically, but spiritually, for my daughter had recently been converted and here she sat with the others magnifying and praising God in another language. My only disappointment was that I could not take part.

Wanda was rapidly catching up with Beulah and I in spiritual understanding.

Every evening she came home from work and spent her hour in our prayer room which we all shared.

"Lord," I thought, "this is beyond my understanding. Here I've known about the pentecostal experience all my life and still haven't received it. But my wife and daughter knew nothing and here they are 'speaking with other tongues' and praying with me, trying to help *me* receive. Surely, Lord, I will receive soon."

It was now May, 1958, and by this time Wanda began to join in with Beulah each night at service tarrying with me until I literally wore myself out. Already the Lord was using them in the gifts of the Spirit. Beulah was teaching, Wanda was preaching. I found that they were beginning to teach me.

I closed my eyes briefly, and let out a sigh. I could almost hear their voices now, "You must let the Spirit speak. It's so easy. Just speak as He gives the utterance. Remember, on the day of Pentecost they began to speak in tongues as the Spirit gave them utterance."

A few mornings later (I now had the downtown route, the best route in the Bluebird Pie Co.), I was driving down Webster Street in the company truck when the word *Shandah* came to my mind with a strong impulse to repeat it. In fact, I almost bit my tongue to keep it from rolling out.

I pondered the situation for a few minutes,

that same scripture running through my mind, "and they spake with other tongues as the Spirit gave them utterance" (Acts 2:4).

Was it possible that the Lord was giving me an utterance? Surely, after all my tarrying, it couldn't be this easy!

The word kept resounding in my head. I was afraid to say it because I was sure that I had heard a good sister in the church speak that same word in the Spirit and it might not be of God if I spoke it too.

I began to talk seriously to the Lord, "Now, Lord, I am going to say that word. There's no one around to hear. If it is from You, please let me know in some way. But, Lord, if it isn't You, please forgive me. Now, here I go, Lord."

So, before I lost my nerve, I repeated quickly, *"SHANDAH."* Immediately ten or twelve more words followed in rapid succession. I was amazed. Where did these strange words come from? My, they sure made me feel good. Such a sweet release spread all over me with the speaking of those words. It was so wonderful that I slammed on the brakes of my truck and pulled over to the side of the road.

I began to talk to the Lord again, "That was really good, Lord. I want to try that again. Now I don't want to offend You, Lord, so You let me know if it's not You. Here I go again, Lord."

Again I repeated, *"SHANDAH"* and more words followed rapidly, and with them came the dawn of understanding. His presence had been there all the time. Somehow, I had gotten the idea that God had to knock me down, take out my tongue and do all the talking. I learned it is fifty-fifty. *He* gives the utterance and *I* do the speaking.

Oh, when I think of all the blessing I had missed by failing to simply accept the Holy Ghost by faith. Now I realize how foolish I was to think that I had to spend hours of labor and travail to make myself worthy of this experience. I had failed to understand that it was a *gift* "given to you and your children and all that are afar off as many as the Lord our God shall call" (Acts 2:39).

Chapter Twelve

TELL-A-VISION

"The Lord showed me someone here is supposed to give fifty dollars in the offering tonight and if you refuse, the Lord is going to put a cancer on you." The threatening tone of the pastor sent chills through every God-fearing believer in attendance.

Such pronouncements began to cause an uneasiness in the congregation.

Beulah and I would often lay in bed at night and discuss the situation, for we had brought many new Christians to church and knew that they were looking to us for understanding. If we accepted this harsh ministry of fear without love, the fate of their souls was our responsibility.

It had all been so wonderful until lately. We had been looking at everything through rose-colored glasses as new Christians are apt to do, but suddenly, it was if our eyes were opened.

We were afraid to tell Wanda after just so recently bringing her into pentecost, but much to our amazement she began to tell us what God had shown her.

One night when God moved on the congregation she stood to her feet and prophesied, "Be not afraid My people. The pastor is deceiving you," and went on to reveal some amazing facts.

She and Beulah, of course, were called on the carpet and told they had a spirit of witchcraft. I feared for them, but they left there rejoicing and praising God. We realized then that God had been teaching us through what we jokingly called a "School of Hard Knocks."

We didn't graduate with any theology, but, we had a degree in "kneeology," acquired through hours of prayer.

It was quite a blow to discover that everyone who attends church isn't necessarily a Christian. We had had a great deal of fear put into us by prophecy until God began to show us that all prophecy does not come from His Spirit. His word must always be coupled with love.

But God had put us there to learn, and learn we did, the hard way. He had shown us things going on behind the scenes and it was quite a shock.

Thus we now found ourselves looking for a new church home. As we prayed and waited for the Lord to direct us, knowing we could not drift from place to place, but needed roots, I was drawn more and more to visit a small church not far from home. I found that I liked both the church and the pastor.

It was new, with a very small congregation, and as I told Wanda and Beulah about it I found myself trying to persuade them that this would be the best place for us to settle down.

There were no young people there and Wanda wasn't too excited about that because she had just met Wayne (now her husband) and she wanted them to have other young people to fellowship with. Then the Lord gave her a dream in which she saw the pastor and a large group of young people over which she would be leader.

It worked just as the Lord showed her. Before long the church began to grow and my wife was given a class to teach and my daughter was preaching and teaching. I was asked to serve on the church Board of Deacons. It seemed as if we were all set for life.

I thought to myself, "My, I'm just the luckiest fellow in the world to have my whole family working for God and being used by Him in a supernatural way."

I was content just being the breadwinner, playing my guitar and going to church regularly. My new route caused a change in my work schedule. Now I went to work at three-thirty in the morning, therefore an afternoon nap was necessary, especially if I wanted to attend church at night.

It was during those hours of rest that God began to direct my life through dreams and visions. Little did I realize that God was beginning to teach me so that I might have faith for the miraculous. Some of my early revelations seemed trivial and at times amusing, but it was God's way of teaching me.

"What would you think if a chipmunk wearing black-rimmed glasses intruded into your sleep?" I asked Beulah upon awakening.

Amused, we chuckled together and she said, "Well, I wouldn't know what to make of it."

I began to describe it to her, "It was the cutest little thing, short and fat, with brown fur. It sat there with its feet up in the air and its eyes staring at me. You know what else was strange, the right lens of the glasses was broken into three pieces all held together by scotch tape."

"What else did it do?" Beulah quizzed.

"Nothing, it just stood up on its hind legs and chattered away. Why would I have such a dream? Could it possibly mean anything?"

"Well, maybe it will have something to do with church tonight," she suggested.

Sure enough, the lady who had just walked into church was someone I had never seen before. She was about fifty-five or sixty years old and her dress was the color of the fur of the little chipmunk, but most amazing, was the fact that she had on glasses exactly like those I had seen in my dream, black-rimmed, broken lens, scotch tape and all.

I thought to myself, "This is no coincidence!"

I was sitting on the platform playing my guitar and it was hard not to continually stare at the woman during the course of the song service.

With that portion of the service concluded, our good pastor asked, "Does anyone have a testimony for the Lord?"

Seizing the opportunity, the lady quickly stood to her feet and in a high-pitched abrasive voice droned on incessantly for what seemed to be at least half-an-hour.

The main theme of her testimony was the self-exalting description of the special anointing of God on her. I was reminded of "sounding brass and tinkling cymbals."

Casting a questioning glance toward my wife, Beulah smiled smugly and nodded.

On Easter, 1959, my daughter came to me with a question I had never considered before.

"Daddy, will you speak for me in youth service about water baptism? The program book that I am using suggested that a deacon of the church give the teaching on baptism."

"No, honey," I excused myself, "I can't speak. I'd have a hard time thinking of anything to say. I'm like Moses, I have a speech impediment. When I get self-conscious, I get my words twisted."

But she quoted the Scriptures to me, "You want to be a New Testament deacon, don't you? You've been praying and asking God to make you one. The Bible says, you, as a deacon must be apt to teach."

Now that really shook me up.

"Okay, okay," I said. "I'll pray about it. I'll ask the Lord to show me."

Little did I realize what was about to take place. I prayed and asked for God's direction, and feeling confident that He had heard me, I laid down for my Sunday nap.

Immediately, my spiritual eyes were opened. I looked to my left and standing there about eighteen inches away was a man like no one I had ever seen before, for He was not made of flesh and bones. He had the shape of a man who was made of consuming fire the color of amber.

Fear fell upon me as I lay there and looked at him. He said one word, *"Speak!"*

I awoke instantly and jumped out of bed. I was so excited that I could hardly contain myself.

Then I thought, "Wait a minute! If you tell that to anyone, they'll think you're crazy. I don't know of anyone ever seeing anything like that before."

So I calmed myself down and went back to bed. No sooner had I done so, when the spiritual being appeared to me again. He stood there a few minutes and let me look at him.

Again I realized there was nothing fleshly about him, I could see no eyes or nose, only outlines. This was a spiritual being who consisted entirely of fire.

He repeated, *"Speak!"*

I came to myself, saturated with the power of God. I could no longer stay in that bed. I had to tell someone.

I pulled on my clothes hastily, yelling, "Beulah, honey, have I got something to tell you. I've just seen an angel of the Lord."

She came running in from where she had been studying her Bible.

The words tumbled out excitedly as I tried to describe to her what had just transpired. "But can this be real?" I earnestly inquired of Beulah, now sceptical of what I had seen. "I've never heard of anyone seeing anything like that before, have you?"

"Let's see if the Bible says something about it," she replied.

We eagerly searched for scriptures on fire. To my amazement I found that God was a consuming fire. I was even more overwhelmed when I found that the vision I had seen was just like the description Ezekiel gave in the first chapter of his book.

Trembling excitedly, I told my daughter when she got home, with an eagerness in my voice, "Okay, honey, I'll speak for you next Saturday night."

Immediately I began studying for my first sermon. I ran all the references in my Bible that I could find on water baptism. I wanted so to do well; therefore, I decided to fast that week also.

"Honey," I announced to Beulah when I came out of my room from prayer before the service that Saturday evening, "guess what? I've been looking at God's television again."

I think she was as thrilled as I was, for all of this was so new to us.

I began to relate to her what had just happened. I had seen myself speaking before the congregation and then realized that I could see and name sicknesses and diseases in people's bodies. To confirm the sickness in one person, I saw a birth mark that would normally be hidden by their clothing.

Another person appeared before me lying on a cot with a sheet pulled up over her. She spoke to me, "Brother Cliff, I want you to look at this place on my body. Doctors have been testing me for a year and do not know what this rash is."

Then I heard a voice from behind me speak as I observed her, "That is a Moabitess."

Upon hearing this, I came to myself and woke up.

I related to my wife as we prepared for church that evening, "Honey, what would you do about these visions? Do you think they are for the service tonight?"

She replied dubiously, "Well, I don't know. I think I would find out if it is the Lord first."

I was left with an uncertainty, but felt I should "try the spirits and see if it be of God."

After my message, I asked, "Is there anyone here with a birthmark?" I began to describe the mark as if it were on my own body pointing to the position.

Immediately a person raised her hand and said, "That is right. I have one like that."

I was thrilled as we prayed for her. Then I decided to try another one of the visions. "There is another person here who has fainting spells and blacks out."

I had seen the face of that person in my vision and when she raised her hand, I knew that this was from the Lord. That gave me even more confidence, so I decided to try the last one although I wasn't sure what to do about the person being a Moabitess.

I said with a positive tone, "There is a person here who has a rash on her stomach which she has had for a year. She does not know what it is although doctors have treated her."

A rather large sister jumped to her feet,

"That's me, Brother Cliff. But how could you know it? I have not told anyone here. Only God could have told you."

I prayed for her and she was healed. I did not tell her the second part of the vision, what the Lord had called the condition, for I didn't understand it myself. I learned later through Bible references that being a Moabitess meant intermarriage between brothers and sisters which was evident in her family history.

Since that day when I saw the angel of the Lord as a fire on Easter Sunday, 1959, there have been many times that I felt that same Presence... always on my left side. It's like standing beside an open fireplace on a chilly day. And, upon each manifestation of his presence, a miracle of healing is performed.

I was secretly thrilled and excited but totally incapable of explaining it to people. Sometimes I tested that Presence by saying to someone, "Why don't you sit down in my seat for just a moment?"

The very moment they would sit down where I had just been sitting and playing my guitar upon the platform, the power of God would surge through them and they would jump up with an exclamation, "Surely there must have been an angel here, for I feel the extraordinary power of God!"

Still others have related to me that they have seen this angel beside me.

And this was not my only contact with God's supernatural power.

As I continued to be faithful to the Lord, still playing my guitar in the service, paying my tithes, serving on the Board, and never missing attendance one night at church, God continued to be faithful to me.

One time for twenty-one consecutive days, as I would rest each afternoon, I would receive either a dream or a vision. God would reveal some particular thing that was going to take place, such as a healing, how many would attend the service, or the pastor's chosen message. Many times He would reveal to me that there was going to be a special speaker for the evening. The pastor had not announced that this speaker would be there and it would be a surprise to all but myself.

It wasn't long before God taught me another very important lesson. After twenty-one days of these special revelations, I started getting a big head.

"Now I have it made," I thought proudly to myself.

Then God put a pin in my balloon to burst my pride. I was resting one afternoon and behold, I had another revelation. In this I saw my own casket. I saw myself standing outside of it, ready, willing, and waiting for the funeral service to start.

I said to myself, "Now when they start the funeral, I'll get into the casket, lie down and let them bury me."

As I observed the casket, I looked to the right of it and there stood five concrete blocks, the ends of them turned towards me. I marveled at the size of them and thought, "Five. Why that means my funeral will be in five days!"

I woke up with quite a different feeling running through me, one of dread and fear. I still had the five cement blocks and the casket on my mind.

I thought to myself, "This is Wednesday, so on Sunday I will die."

I was afraid to tell anyone this new revelation. All week long I lived in fear. Saturday rolled around and I nearly panicked. I expected to die the next day.

I began to cry out to God, "Oh, God, I'm so afraid to die, even if You *were* the One that showed me it's my time!"

The Spirit of the Lord came upon me as I prayed so desperately and then His peace settled in my heart. I waited on the Lord and finally God began to get through to me.

"Why am I afraid?" I thought to myself. "Fear is not from God. Fear is from the devil. Why should God show me that I am going to die and then allow me to be afraid?"

Sound reasoning took hold of me. I stood to my feet and rebuked the devil, "You get away from me! I will not die."

Then I realized that I had been tested. God was trying to show me that every dream and vision wasn't always from Him and I must put each of them to the test. I had to be scriptural in everything that I did.

I learned from that particular vision that there was an unbreakable rule that said that the Spirit and the Word must always agree.

And, as I continued working for the Lord, He still continued to teach me through dreams and visions. I called it looking at God's tell-a-vision.

You see a vision and then tell it to the one who needs it and it comes to pass!

Chapter Thirteen

"X-RAY" VISION

"Oh, no, not again!" I muttered, frustrated at the pain which persisted in my chest. I had tried for several weeks to ignore it thinking perhaps it was only the results left from a cough and cold I had had.

It would begin with a small pain in my chest, close to my heart, and then spread to a larger area across my back.

I finally decided that I should see a doctor. The old fear of heart trouble rose up within me, although this was a different kind of pain.

But, all the doctor could tell me was that he thought it might be a nerve under pressure. So, I decided to go to another doctor, who diagnosed it as something else. The only thing that they had both agreed upon was the fact they should put me in the hospital and run some tests if it got any worse.

That night I lay in bed, tossing and turning,

trying to move from to side to side without awakening Beulah. I found I could not sleep on my left side or my stomach because the pain would become so severe that when my heart beat it shook the bed. I was fear-stricken.

"Oh, Lord," I sobbed softly, trying not to let my emotions overcome me and awaken Beulah. "Lord, You know my condition better than I do. If I go back to the doctor, he will likely send me to the hospital. If he does, I will lose work, and if I lose work, I won't make any money. If I don't make any money, I won't be able to pay my tithes. If I don't pay any tithes, You'll get no glory. Therefore, either You heal me or I'll be like old Jacob in the Bible; I'll just pull my legs up under me and I'll die."

I knew that my healing had to come from God and I continued wrestling with Him, reasoning that I needed His healing power to bring glory and honor to His name.

"Lord, if I don't get healed, I won't be in church and therefore You can get no glory from that. But there's one thing about it, Lord, I don't want to make a rash promise. Tomorrow I may have a headache and I may take an aspirin. I don't know about my faith for those things tomorrow. But, this time, either You heal me of this condition or I'll die."

I felt that God knew I really meant what I was saying. Therefore, I kept petitioning Him. I reminded Him, "Lord, I've done all I know to do. I've been faithful, I've paid my tithes and You know it."

I kept glancing at the clock every so often for sleep had escaped me.

It was now two-thirty in the morning. Whether in a dream or a vision, a soft glow suddenly appeared in the room growing brighter and brighter. Cloaked in the light was an angel of the Lord. I looked at Him in amazement.

"My," I thought to myself, "he must be from the Middle East somewhere!"

He looked as if he had just stepped out of the pages of the New Testament. He was dressed in what appeared to be a kingly garment; a jacket of some sort with a high, wide waist band on the full trousers which were golden brown in color.

But his dress was not what arrested my attention, it was his eyes. They defied description and had the ability to look right through me.

Suddenly, another man appeared on his right side. I turned my eyes from the angel's face to look at the new visitor and was astounded to discover it was me.

The angelic visitor reached his right hand over to the vision of my body and took my heart out. He then thrust it forward so I could examine it.

I stared at it from a distance of about six feet. As I did so, my heart was magnified and I noticed that there was a little red circle drawn on it. Within that red circle was a portion of the vein which appeared to be swollen.

Understanding clicked in my mind as a light switched on in a darkened room. I knew suddenly that he was telling me without words that a blood vessel was about to rupture, and this had been the root of my trouble.

Tranquillity settled over me. I now felt assured that God would heal me.

Joyfully, I said to the angel, "Why, that is me!"

He answered, "Yes."

Many questions rushed through my mind. "That's my heart you have in your hand, isn't it?"

Again he replied, "Yes."

I grew even more excited as the knowledge was confirmed. "Well, is that the trouble there in that red circle?"

"Yes," again affirmative.

"Well, what do I do about it?" I asked in anticipation.

"Get your wife to anoint it."

Upon that statement he disappeared and I came to myself. I jumped out of the bed and right there in the middle of the floor I began dancing and rejoicing. My whole body was vibrating with power. I woke my wife right then.

I usually let her sleep since I left the house at three-thirty each morning, but I had to tell her what had transpired.

"Honey, the Lord is going to heal me. Thank God healing is on the way."

I explained while dressing for work what had happened. She rejoiced with me, secure in the knowledge that God was going to deliver me from this condition.

I went to work that day exuberant. Although I had not slept, I felt refreshed.

My day on the job went very quickly. It was the best day I had ever had. The pain was still there, of course, but I ignored it, for my fear was gone. I knew that soon God would completely heal me, although I did not know what day or what hour.

"God is so mindful of me," I whispered to myself as I went in and out of the stores delivering pies. "Just think, He has sent His angel to me to show me my problem and give me faith to receive my healing."

When I arrived home from work that same afternoon and was sitting at the dinner table, my pastor came around the corner and knocked at the door.

I beckoned him in and invited him to sit down and have lunch with me.

"I've got so much to tell you, you just have to take the time and listen," I told him in excitement.

As I related the vision to him, he too began to rejoice, believing that it was from the Lord and that He was going to heal me.

I couldn't wait. "I know what I want to do," I said. "I want to act out that vision."

Something had just popped into my mind I remembered an evangelist telling me. When you have a vision, and there is a part for you to play, you should act it out.

"Let's go into the living room." I hopped up from the table filled with expectancy.

I pulled out an old hassock that sat in front of my favorite chair. I sat down upon it, for I had expended all my energy by now and ached all over.

My pastor moved to my left side where the angel of the Lord had stood in the vision of the previous night.

My wife then stood on my right side. She acted upon the instructions left by the angel. She took a bottle of olive oil, opened it, and with the tip of her finger covering the top let the oil trickle on her hand. I unbuttoned a few buttons of my shirt. Then she anointed my chest where the pain even now throbbed.

Just as they got ready to pray for me, the power of God came down and hit me in the top of the head. It surged through my body like 10,000 volts of electricity. It was so dynamic and so powerful that my feet and legs jerked out and my body stiffened.

Right at that moment the ache in my chest

went right out the bottom of my feet. The power of God continued to resurge up and down my body two or three more times.

They had just reached out their hands to pray for me when I jumped up and yelled, "I'm healed, I'm healed! You don't need to pray."

We rejoiced and shouted together for all the pain was gone, every symptom.

Three days later the pain returned with a stubborn persistence. But I had prepared myself, for I had been taught that the devil often returns to test your faith.

"Satan, you get away from me in Jesus' name! You're not coming back because I was healed last Monday at two o'clock." I stated positively to him again, "You need not bring those symptoms back here and make me think I've got that condition again. God has healed me and that is that. I do not have heart trouble anymore!"

With this statement of faith, every symptom fled my body. That was in 1962 and to this day I have not had another symptom.

Chapter Fourteen

NEVER TOO LATE

God continued to bless me with dreams and visions. Some of them came to pass immediately while others remained a mystery for a long time. Some dreams had spiritual significance while others had practical value.

Following the resignation of our pastor, a new pastor was elected to take his place. Under his leadership the church progressed to the place where the present facilities were inadequate. Soon plans were formulated to expand by adding a new sanctuary.

God was in this building program. Our new pastor's past experience as a contract builder proved to be of tremendous value. The physical construction such as the masonry, the carpentry, the roofing, the plaster board, all were so well-planned due to his past experience, that, in my estimation, we could have hauled the scraps of lumber, dry wall, etc. away in several wheel barrow loads.

There was one area, however, in which no one had the necessary training. The pastor gave me the task of installing the new public address system. Having only limited knowledge from my experiences playing the electric guitar and tinkering around with my own tape recorder, I was simply not qualified for this important job.

God saw my willingness to tackle it. Yet as I gave it much thought and prayed about it and asked questions of qualified men, I was still totally in the dark. But God was not in the dark, His knowledge even extends to public address systems.

In a dream, God showed me where to put every wire in the ceiling, where to place each outlet, where to place the speaker, where to put the amplifier, even where to place the tables in the control room so tape recorders could operate during the service.

The dry wall had not yet been installed in the new sanctuary, so I climbed through the bare rafters placing the wires exactly as I had seen them in my dream. When the dry wall ceiling was installed the speakers were set in place and the P.A. system was connected to the electrical source. I anxiously flipped the switch, waiting until the tubes' amber glow showed that the system had warmed up. I picked up a microphone and gave the usual "Testing—1-2-3—."

"Glory!" I heard the pastor shout as the sound carried throughout the building.

It had worked on the first try!

Throughout the building program, the anticipated completion date was late spring, 1962. The pastor spoke several times of planning the dedication service for May.

When I told him that the Lord had showed me in a dream that there would be snow on the ground when the church was dedicated, I could tell by the look on his face that his opinion had remained unchanged . . . May was the date.

The building program continued through April, through May, through June, on through the summer into late September. Dedication day was finally set for October 22, 1962.

Upon awakening, I eagerly prepared myself for this long-awaited event. Dedication day had finally come. We were to officially present the fruit of our labor to the service of the Master. We were so proud; the final result had been beyond our expectation.

And the pastor would drawl in his native Kentucky tongue, squinting his eyes and smiling, "It's a lo-ve—l-ly san-c—tu-ary."

As I went to the bathroom to shave, I drew back the curtain. Lying softly on the front lawn was a blanket of snow about two inches deep.

When I saw the pastor at Sunday School

that morning, it was hard to keep from saying, "See, I told you so."

Each day as I rested after work, the Lord continued to speak to me through dreams. But, now His messages seemed to be taking a specific direction.

There was one common theme to all of them. I began to see myself in Bible school.

"Now Lord," I would argue, "I'm too old to go to Bible school. Who ever heard of a forty-eight-year-old man going to Bible school?"

I wasn't being rebellious, it just seemed improbable.

"Could it be that God is actually calling me to the ministry?" I asked myself. "Well, I'll just prove God and see what happens," I finally decided.

From all the evidence, I had suspected that God actually was calling me to the ministry, but being cautious by nature I needed additional confirmation.

The Lord is faithful. He is the rewarder of them that diligently seek Him. Attending a revival alone in a strange church, I was impressed to join the line of believers as they were invited to come forward for special prayer. The evangelist was on furlough from his missionary work in Brazil.

As he moved along the line praying for various people, occasionally giving a word of knowledge or prophecy to bolster their faith, my confidence in him as a man of God took root.

When he came to me, he asked, "What's wrong with you, brother?"

Feeling this was the time to put my previous confirmations to the test, I smiled and said, "You tell me."

Sensing my sincerity, he studied my face momentarily, then reaching out and laying his hand upon my head and closing his eyes, he began to speak in tongues and prophesy, "My son, I have called you. I have laid My hand upon you. You are to preach My Word. You go and I will go with you and I will anoint you."

It was tremendous. As I began to weep with joy, I realized that here was a total stranger confirming what God had already been showing me through my dreams.

As I would attend other churches and situations would arise which demanded tact on the part of the pastor, the Lord would speak to me and say, "When you are a pastor, this is the way you should handle the situation."

I was learning by observation.

"Here I am—putting God to the test again," I said to Beulah, my sister Orpha, and her husband Dude as we sat waiting for the service to begin at the First Pentecostal Church of Xenia, Ohio.

We had heard much about the atmosphere at the Xenia church being akin to heaven and had come to know Reverend Brooks through his radio ministry. We also had confidence in him because of his reputation among the area pastors.

The building was crowded when the service began. We sat half-way back soaking in all the blessings. We joined in with the boisterous song leader, singing and clapping our hands and feeling right at home.

The Spirit of the Lord moved upon a lady sitting on the platform. She gave a dynamic utterance in an unknown tongue.

The audience sat in holy reverence awaiting the Spirit to move upon a believer to give an interpretation.

From the moment the Spirit had begun to move, I was overwhelmed. Again, I felt the manifestation of the Lord as on the night of my initial baptism in the Holy Ghost. It was as though God unzipped my chest and allowed a good, warm tropical-like rain to saturate me inside.

I knew the message was for me. Standing at the microphone, Brother Brooks gave the interpretation, "Son, I have called you. You go and I will go with you and I will anoint you. I'll send them unto you from the Nazarenes, the Presbyterians, the Catholics, the Church of Christ and even the Jehovah's Witnesses."

Exhilarated by the words which had added

weight to the belief that I was truly called to preach, I was further thrilled to find that those who were riding in the car with me had known from the moment the message began that it was for me.

Having been in the pulpit only seven times previously to minister from the Word of God, I was quite uncertain of my ability to fulfill the calling.

"Lord, I don't want to embarass Your work. I don't want to hang out a sign to do something for God, saying that I am to have a church unless You prove it," I prayed.

Then, in early May, 1965, while asleep one afternoon, I was in the Spirit. I was in a huge barn along with several other young preachers as they were graduating from Bible school. I stood to one side watching the young men walk up to an old prophet who gave each a coin and a sandwich and said, "Thus, saith the Lord, You shall go to the north, the south, the east, and the west."

"You are next," a Voice behind me said.

I awoke uncertain as to how I should feel. The old fear haunted me that I would fail in my effort to please God. It had not yet been revealed to what field of ministry I was being called.

"Lord, what is the ministry that You want me to have?" I earnestly entreated. "I am convinced that You are going to use me, but do You want to use me as a witness on the streets? Shall I be a teacher? Do You want me to be a missionary, an evangelist, a pastor? Lord, You're going to have to show me."

The Bible says, "Ask, and ye shall receive."

True to His Word, one night in late 1965, as I lay my head on the pillow in sleep, I dreamed that I went to a Bible bookstore in downtown Dayton. There I saw two signs with the letters in capitals spelling, "CLERGY."

In my dream, I purchased both of them, reasoning that these were the type of signs that pastors attach to their license plates.

Since my pie route was downtown, it was convenient for me to stop at the particular store I had seen in my dream the next day. And as a confirmation, they had two such signs in stock. I purchased them as an act of faith.

Here I was forty-eight years old and called into the ministry. It's never too late!

Chapter Fifteen

SPYING OUT THE LAND

The Vandalia area seemed to beckon us. There were no full-gospel churches in that little town just a few miles north of Dayton. It had gained the reputation of being the local "Crossroads of America" because of the intersections of the Dixie Highway, Route 25 and Old National Road, Route 40.

Beulah and I spent many hours driving around, combing the community searching for a building which would accomodate a pioneer church.

We kept our plans a secret. We did not want to influence any of our family and friends to feel obligated to join this venture with us.

At the same time that the Lord was dealing with me concerning my call into the ministry, He was also creating a discomfort in our local church. It seemed that since the day of the dedication, the atmosphere of the new sanctuary seemed to stifle the liberty and movement of the Spirit. The mode of worship had so much order, with its pomp and dignity, that we, with our southern upbringing and way of worship, no longer felt comfortable.

It soon became evident that many of the faithful ones who had weathered the storm of the growing years were beginning to filter out into other churches and were being replaced by those who were better educated or held more influential positions in the community. Although I loved the church, the people and the pastor, I no longer felt comfortable. I began to feel more like a maturing eaglet.

As the mother eagle stirreth up her nest removing the soft lining, so God was stirring up my nest. Sometimes we have to feel the pricks and sticks to encourage us to try our own wings.

We did not want to create a discord among those still in attendance, so we quietly went about "spying out the land," looking for a building and praying for God's direction.

Unable to find a building to rent, God showed me that we were to do it the hard way, purchase a place and build by faith.

I began then to understand why God had given me so many dreams and visions and allowed them to come to pass. He was teaching me to have the faith to follow His instructions.

"God, show me where to go," I prayed.

Then one afternoon as I was resting, he gave me a glimpse of the future.

In a dream, Beulah and I were going north through a lovely valley. As we drove, we looked to our left and there sat a beautiful building constructed of blond bricks.

Pointing toward it, I said to her, "Honey, there is where we are going to have a church."

"What are we going to use for people?" she puzzled.

My answer to her was, "If you have something to give, people will come to get it."

Immediately, we were inside the building. There we viewed the layout of the place, its construction, and its beautiful green carpeting.

In that dream, God promised that He would give us special power over unclean spirits. I could see Beulah and I rejoicing.

The dream came to an end shortly, but upon awakening, I had a new outlook for my future. I was very sure that the revelation was from the Lord and that somewhere in the years ahead it would come to pass.

I was edified and elated for the Lord had offered a seemingly unobtainable goal. Like the horse reaching for the elusive carrot dangling before him, I was enticed to keep moving toward its fulfillment.

Chapter Sixteen

GOD'S MONEY IN OTHER POCKETS

That I was called to be a pastor, I was now convinced. Along with the call, God had given me the goal of building a new church. Still missing, however, were two important ingredients, people to pastor, and money with which to build.

One evening as I sat reading the newspaper, the telephone rang. I answered. The voice of a good friend of mine, Bascomb Dorton, resounded through the earpiece, "Cliff, could Christine and I come and see you for a few minutes. I hope you're not busy for we just have to talk to you."

"Sure, come on up," I replied, wondering what was so important that they had to make a special trip to see me in person.

When they arrived, I could tell that they were definitely excited about something.

"Cliff," Bascomb began, "Christine has something she wants to tell you."

She spoke up then, "I had a dream last night that was so real. I was watching you as you walked from building to building looking for a place where we could have church. Then I heard a voice speak to me, 'He is going to build a church. You go help him.'"

When she told me that, I knew more than ever that God was with me and that what God had been telling me was true.

I began rejoicing. God was confirming through them what He had already shown me.

I confessed that I was indeed looking for a building.

"Then we plan to be with you and help you," they both replied immediately.

"I want to have a part in this," Bascomb wept. "I want to give you the first one hundred dollars right now."

I had hardly let them out the door when my telephone rang again. This time it was Brother and Sister Webb who lived down the street from us. Again was the question, "May we come over?"

"Sure," was my reply.

Within a matter of minutes they arrived at the house and knocked. Inviting them in and showing them to a seat, I was very curious about their beaming faces.

Astonishingly enough, Sister Webb spoke up with another of God's revelations, for I knew that they were in the dark about our intentions. "I had a dream last night. I saw you walk through the doorway with a Bible in your hand. There was an angel behind you who said that you were going to be a prophet and a preacher."

Before she could finish, I broke down and cried.

We all sat there with tears streaming down our faces, knowing that only God could have revealed His will concerning me to all these people.

Finally, able to speak without choking up, I began to relate to them from beginning to end all that had transpired. I told them of the other couple who had just left.

Hearing me affirm that God was calling me into the ministry to begin a church, they volunteered, "We have two hundred dollars to help you get started."

I then told my precious mother, who has since been called on to Glory, about my plans.

"Cliff, I want to give you a thousand dollars," she exclaimed excitedly.

"No, Mom, I can't take money from you," I quickly told her. I knew that she could not afford such an amount.

"Yes, you can and you will," she insisted.

There was no point in arguing with Mom. Then I realized that God would bless her for giving and she would grieve if she didn't give.

"All right, Mom," I smilingly submitted. Her confidence in me meant so much.

My faith began to grow by leaps and bounds as I realized that God was supplying us with people who believed in us and would entrust themselves to me to be their pastor.

Our "church treasury" now had a grand total of thirteen hundred dollars.

The time had come when we felt compelled to inform my daughter and son-in-law of our intentions. It was our hopes that they, too, would join us. However, we did not want to pressure them with our parental influence. We knew God could direct them as He had the others.

Because of their discontentment, they had terminated their membership at our old church. They had begun attending a larger church across town where they were trying to get lost in the crowd to wait for God's direction.

I felt assured that God would direct them to unite with us because of a previous statement in a board meeting. The church in the north side at that time was considering a branch church in Vandalia and a number of men pledged their support. Wayne had stated as we sat in the board meeting together, "If anyone goes to Vandalia, I'm going with them."

The plans to establish a branch church in Vandalia never bore fruit. However, even though those plans were cancelled, we still believed that God wanted a full-gospel church in that community.

The pledge of support which was promised to the young minister at that board meeting was not passed on to me. My efforts met with nothing but resistance while attending that church and even for some time thereafter. It became evident that we were going to have to be an independent work.

Thankfully, in the years to come as it was proven that God was in the plan, all differences between these church members and my family were reconciled.

Chapter Seventeen

FAITH WITH WORKS

My wife and I began our search, this time not for rental property, but for land to buy. According to the revelation, we headed north, up North Dixie Drive.

We had gone about five and one-half miles when we passed a little cottage setting off to the left of the roadway nestled in a clump of evergreen hedges beneath a grove of towering locust trees. A *For Sale* sign was standing in the front yard.

"Beulah, write down that realtor's name," I said, slowing the car so she could get all the information.

I quickly turned around and headed home. When we arrived, Sister Betty Webb was coming across the street. We told her about it. Betty became excited after hearing our description. She expressed a desire to see it. She and Beulah decided to drive back up and take a better look at the place.

Unable to find anyone at home, they walked around the dwelling, peeped in the windows, and came back with the report, "It's not big enough. You don't want that!"

But a steady conviction grew within me. I was determined to check out the information anyway. I went over to the phone and began dialing. The phone rang at the other end.

"Is this Harry Lamb?" I asked.

"Yes," was the reply of a kindly voice.

"Could you give me some information concerning the property at 8921 North Dixie Drive?" I asked, praying that it wouldn't be too high.

He replied, "The owners are asking $12,900 for it. And let me tell you this. They will only sell outright. They will not accept a land contract."

I asked hopefully, "Well, then how much of a mortgage will the place carry?"

He answered, "Oh, I suppose about fifty percent."

I quickly figured in my mind that even with the pledges of $1,300 and $400 which Beulah and I had laid aside, we were still about $4,800 short of the necessary fifty percent.

I replied that I wasn't sure we could procure such an amount. But God was our source and Harry Lamb seemed interested in helping us to acquire it. I invited him to come to the house and bring a contract.

"I'll be right there," he promised.

While waiting, I thought to myself, "Now the Lord has shown me that I am going to be a preacher. I know I have not been trained and I really don't feel that I have the proper vocabulary. Most of all, I don't feel worthy, but I'm afraid not to preach after all the things that God has revealed to me."

As I mused about the matter, I felt that this was the time to put my faith into action. I decided we would give the realtor a deposit of $100 and make an offer.

In a few minutes, there was a knock at the door and when Harry Lamb walked in, the Spirit spoke to me, "Tell this man all that is happening to you."

Somewhat reluctantly, I began talking once he was seated. I found myself telling him all about God's dealings with me in dreams and visions and about the prophecies of going into the ministry. I even confessed that I dreaded it because I had not been trained, but that I was afraid to disobey the Lord. I saw tears come into the man's eyes and run down his cheeks.

He looked at me with conviction in his voice and said, "I feel like going home and throwing my television through the window, getting my Bible and going with you."

As our conversation continued, I discovered that this man had Bible school training and was now very involved as a lay minister in his church.

God had sent us a Christian realtor,

someone who would believe in us and one in whom we could have confidence.

As I affixed my signature to the offer to purchase the property, I signed the matter over to the Lord. He alone could help us secure the amount needed for the down payment.

As Brother Lamb left with that important piece of paper in his briefcase, the wheels of Divine Providence were set in motion.

Such anxiety! Such excitement! The rest of that day and the next seemed to go so slowly. I thought only of that little patch of ground on North Dixie Drive. Our step of faith was as one testing the ice on a lake not knowing whether the Lord would uphold us or whether in our venture we would fall through. We had acted without a direct revelation, believing that this transaction was in God's will.

On Sunday night, May 29, 1965, after arriving home from church, I retired for the night. It had been less than thirty-six hours since signing the purchase contract. I fretted about the property and tried to go to sleep. But sleep fled from me! I could do nothing but pray concerning the negotiation.

An Old Testament story kept filtering through my mind. It concerned Jacob's ladder with the angels ascending and descending to heaven. After his night of sleep, he arose and poured oil upon the stone which he had used for a pillow saying, "Surely, the Lord is in this place and I knew it not."

I looked at the clock. It was 2:00 A.M. I knew it was futile to try to sleep as I would have to get up at 3:30 to go to work. I decided to rise and read for the remaining hour until it was time to leave. I reached for my Bible and slipped softly out to the living room and turned on the light, intending to read and study for that period of time.

But reading, too, was impossible. My mind continued to wander to the experience of Jacob and his ladder.

"Lord, are you trying to tell me something?" I pondered prayerfully.

An impulse came to me which seemed preposterous. I couldn't do that. I'd look ridiculous if anyone saw me. After a few moments of wavering, I went to the kitchen and took the bottle of olive oil out of the cabinet.

Dressing hastily, I drove to the property. Very few cars were on the road at that time of the morning. A cloak of slumber enshrouded the northern environs of the suburb through which I passed.

Upon reaching my destination, I pulled up slowly, stopped and got out of the car. I left the car door open so that I could get back in quickly.

"I hope no one sees me," I thought. "After all, I am trespassing. One of the neighbors might awaken, think that I am up to no good, and start shooting."

The thought sent chills down my spine. I hurried to carry out my mission.

Standing majestically at the front of the property was a large walnut tree. Its ominous silhouette seemed to impose itself as a silent sentinel guarding the now darkened property.

Nervously, I removed the cap from the bottle of olive oil. I glanced around to make certain no one was looking. All windows were still dark in the neighborhood. As I poured the smooth-flowing liquid onto the base of the tree, I prayed, "God, as Jacob of old poured oil on the stone, saying, 'Surely, God hath been in this place,' I am pouring this oil and following his example. God, surely You are going to meet me in this place."

Quickly, I climbed back into the car. I had left the engine running to insure a fast get away. As I pulled away, I felt very relieved. My relief was twofold: First, my deed had gone undetected. Second, I had followed what I believed to be the urging of the Spirit.

It was now time for me to go to work. I rested on the promises of God knowing He had seen my act of faith and would confirm it.

Five days later, still waiting for an answer from the realtor, I had a dream. In it I was standing in front of that house with an old dirt pick in my hands. I began digging and soon uncovered a well.

A number of people who I thought were unusually beautiful stood watching, smiling approvingly. One of them asked, "What are you doing here?"

"I'm going to build a church," I answered.

The dream ended as I awoke.

The next night I dreamed the same dream, but it continued beyond the previous one. At the point that I uncovered the well, to my amazement I found a pipe protruding from it with a faucet on top. As I dug around and uncovered the facet, I thought to myself, "My what an unusual well with a faucet on the top. I've never seen one like that."

Then I turned my head to look at all the people who were watching me. In the background about a block to the north, I saw a 1964 Chevrolet Impala sedan with a white body and blue top pulling into the driveway of a house across the street. When the car stopped, a man got out and went into the house. The people watching me asked, "Who is that?"

I replied, "That's Ronald Caperton. I know him well. He used to attend a large formal church and was unsaved, but I helped pray him through to the baptism of the Holy Ghost. He married a cousin of mine."

When I awoke and came out of the vision, I knew that everything I had seen was true. Ronald Caperton *did* live in that direction and had married my cousin. I *had* helped pray him through to the Holy Ghost. This had completed my dream of the previous night and served to confirm it.

I remembered according to the Bible that Joseph had said, "If you dream a dream twice, it is sure and for certain and will shortly come to pass." (see Genesis 41:32).

There could be no question about it. God was going to make a way to purchase the property. But with that assurance arose another apprehension. I knew then that soon I would have to prove my ability to preach and minister to a congregation. That scared me more than trusting God for the property.

Each day brought us closer to the expiration date of the purchase agreement for which we needed the balance of the down payment. We had finally scraped together all but $800. My wife had borrowed $3,000 from Kroger's Credit Union. I had borrowed $1,000 on my car. Other friends had also given money to us, but at last we had run short of resources. Concern for the amount still needed to complete the down payment weighed heavily on my mind as I retired for bed the night before the expiration date of our contract to purchase.

While asleep, whether in a vision or a dream, I was carried to downtown Dayton. The Lord showed me a bird's eye view of the buildings facing both sides of Main Street near the Third Street intersection.

From my vantage point, I was looking

toward the west side. As I gazed on the scene, my eyes came to rest on a building adjoining the north side of the Dayton Power and Light Building.

The Spirit spoke to me, "In there, is all the money you'll ever need."

I awoke knowing that if we were in God's will, He would supply the need.

I called Mr. Lamb and told him hesitantly, "I'm sorry, but we lack $800 of the down payment."

He responded, "Get dressed. Get your coat on. I'm picking you up in a few minutes. We're going downtown together."

Not knowing what he had in mind, I followed his instructions. We arrived at State Fidelity on the west side of Main Street in downtown Dayton. I was speechless when I arrived and saw the loan institution with which Brother Lamb had made an appointment was situated just where I had seen it the night before! We were ushered into a large office and offered a seat. What followed I will never forget.

Harry Lamb began talking, briefly explaining to the vice-president what had happened, "Gene, Cliff and his wife have been praying. They feel that God wants them to start a church on this property and what's more I believe them. They lack $800 though for the down payment."

Then he pressed the matter further, "Look,

can you go beyond the appraisal, or somehow strengthen it?"

The vice-president told Harry then, "The appraisers set the loan value at $6,500, but I'll tell you what I will do. I'll take a chance on what you're saying and help them. I'll put up $400, and that will only leave them $400 short."

Harry responded excitedly, "Then I'll put up the other $400."

I was dumbfounded. I had never heard businessmen talking like this before. God was moving for me. Later, I learned why. Harry explained to me that businessmen's prayer meetings were being conducted at the bank in downtown Dayton. Then I realized that God had men in important places and was using them to help me.

Shortly after the closing date, when the property was finally in our name, we were curious about the condition of the inside of the house. During the period of negotiations, I had not been permitted by the owners to see the inside, but because of the direction of God, we had purchased it anyway.

I was getting excited and anxious now to begin our work for the Lord. My wife and I went to the house and knocked on the door and I asked, "May we come in?"

The lady replied, "No, you can't. We have thirty days in which to vacate and you have to wait until we leave, then you can see it."

Since she wouldn't allow us in, I asked, "Would it be all right if we walked around on the property and looked it over?"

"Well, it's your property. Of course, you can walk around on it," she replied haughtily. With that she shut the door in our faces.

We walked around behind the house noting everything. Then suddenly I stopped in surprise.

"Beulah, look here!" I exclaimed.

My faith leaped to its peak. I was overwhelmed, for right there in front of me was the funny looking well with the faucet on top that I had seen in my dream.

My heart bubbled over. We were still moving in the way that God was revealing—step-by-step, dream-by-dream.

Chapter Eighteen

MOVING ON THE PREMISES

No longer did we have to stand on the promises, we were now moving onto the premises. We had eagerly awaited the day that the previous owner would move. Immediately, we began work, knocking out partitions between the living room, kitchen, and bedroom to enlarge the area to accommodate as many people as possible. When we finished, we had an auditorium which could comfortably seat forty-five people.

We had one separate room left to serve as a nursery and classroom and one restroom. A curtain could be pulled across one side to provide another room, giving us a total area for three classrooms on Sunday morning.

We worked most of the summer on that place preparing it as a sanctuary for souls that needed God. It got so hot one afternoon that I decided, "Lord, we need an air conditioner. I'm beginning to believe You for a crowd to fill this place and it's awfully hot in here."

I wanted people to be able to worship in comfort so that their minds would not be distracted by the heat.

Later that day, I stopped at a store to price an air conditioner. I knew we couldn't afford to pay cash so I decided to buy it on credit.

I had just arrived home and was telling Beulah of my intentions when the phone rang.

Mom's voice rang out with smothered laughter. She began teasing me, prolonging what she wanted to tell me.

Finally, she said, "Cliff, I was praying today and the Lord spoke to me and told me to buy an air conditioner for the church building."

I was certainly surprised, to say the least, for this idea had only presented itself this day and here was my mother offering to buy what I had just been praying for. But I knew she couldn't afford it.

"Mom," I told her, "you can't. You've already given enough; too much in fact."

"No," she said, "that's that. I'm going to buy it."

I knew once again that there was no stopping her and certainly God was in it. He must have laid the matter on her heart. Her willingness to give to God provided us with better working conditions and enabled us to progress much faster toward the work that

God was to start in just a few short weeks.

Soon after the purchase of the property, word spread that we were making a church out of the house. Some of the neighbors objected strongly. One neighbor, who at first had seemed very friendly and even offered to allow us the use of any of his tools in remodeling, turned against us when he discovered we were going to use the building for a place of worship. It was he who drew up a petition and circulated it throughout the neighborhood to try to prevent us. Some signed, most didn't. God was for us and those who were against us failed.

One day, I stopped to chat with that neighbor. "I'd like to invite you to visit us," I said.

He grew very agitated and exploded angrily, "I don't like Billy Graham."

I softly replied, "Well, I do."

Even more hatefully, he stated, "I don't like Oral Roberts."

Again I answered quietly, "I do."

I got the message. He was telling me in no uncertain terms that he did not want any preachers around him.

One of the next times I spoke to him, he plainly stated that fact. My reply to him was merely that that was between him and God.

He continued to do many things to harass our work, but like Nehemiah I was too busy building to stop and argue. He cursed us many times and threatened us until he really became a thorn in our side.

We were to learn eventually that God was already working for us to remove this thorn.

With the partitions in place, the brown-speckled tile sparkling on the floor and the smell of fresh paint filling the air, the small room was vaguely beginning to take on the appearance of a church, except that we now needed seating.

The biggest problem was that we had no money.

Then God proved Himself to us again. Bluebird Pie Company began making special occasion cakes. To promote the new product, a contest was started between the route salesmen of the company. The one selling the most cakes within a thirty-day period would receive 25,000 Top Value stamps as a prize.

I began to pray about winning. "Now, Lord, if I had those 25,000 stamps, I could use them to get eight or nine folding chairs for our church building."

God began to move for me, for without any effort on my part, people in the stores would come up to me and ask, "Say, do you sell birthday cakes?"

I sold enough to win the first prize over 164 other drivers. My foreman was so excited that he gave me the 5,000 Top Value stamps which he had won for being the division manager of the winning salesman.

My wife was so enthusiastic about all that God was doing for us that one day, while running the cash register at Krogers, she began to tell a customer about winning the stamps and the purpose for which they were being used.

He was thrilled. "I have 5,000 Top Value Stamps myself," he said. "Let me give them to you, too."

Then, without any soliciting, three other people came to us. Each offered 5,000 more stamps. This brought us to a grand total of 40,000 stamps which meant twelve folding chairs in all.

We now had some chairs for our lone Sunday School room, but still needed pews for the sancutary. Each evening, I searched the want ads.

One evening, as I quickly scanned the classified section, one small listing caught and held my attention.

I tore the ad from the paper.

"Beulah, I finally found some church seats listed!" I shouted.

I should have expected it, for God had been with us all the way and now that the time had come to put the pews in the building, here was the necessary provision.

We hopped in the car and drove to Miamisburg, Ohio, and found that a church was dissolving and was selling all their equipment. The pews they showed us were the old style theatre seats, and they wanted one hundred dollars for ten sections of them.

My wife began to witness to the man about our new work in the Vandalia area and how God was blessing us. When we left there, we had not only the pews, but also the platform, some building material, the pulpit, and the piano, all for the original one hundred dollars.

We were amazed at the way God was providing for us.

As we moved closer to the day we would open the doors of the church for ministry, I began to consider my hopeful dreams of the new life God was opening to me.

"Give me your tired, your poor,
Your huddled masses,
Yearning to breathe free,
The wretched refuse of your teeming shores,
Send these, the homeless tempest tossed to
me.
I lift my lamp beside the golden door."

These words by Emma Lazarus found written on a tablet at the base of the Statue of Liberty in New York harbor perhaps best expressed my feelings as I stood on the threshold of my new ministry preparing to become pastor of the yet unborn church in Murlin Heights.

My prayer was, "Lord, I'm going out there and answer Your call and if You have any sheep that have been beaten and abused by some mean preacher, You send them to me and I'll do my best to show them that I love them."

I so wanted our church to serve as a refuge for those who felt like we had, that they did not fit in churches where the gospel was used as a verbal whip, and where they were exposed to gimmicks and pressures to fleece them of their money. I wanted to be the kind of shepherd who would lead his flock and not drive them, and pour oil in their wounds instead of salt. If there was one word that I wished to use to describe the atmosphere of the Murlin Heights church, it was LOVE.

Meanwhile, the day we were to have our first worship service was fast approaching. And I knew that I was going to have to start producing. Many of my friends and family voiced their confidence in my calling to become a pastor. However, that same confidence did not completely fill my heart. What if no one came to our new church? What if the First Pentecostal Church of Murlin Heights (we had decided to call it that for the obvious reason that it *was* the first pentecostal church in Murlin Heights) remained empty? And so I prayed:

"God, we've got the building ready, the pews, the piano, the pulpit. Now we need the people." I continued to seek the Lord. "We have a few promises, but we have no firm commitments. Surely, Lord, if You gave me this place, You'll send me people to pastor."

"Dad, let me tell you the dream I had last night," my daughter exclaimed as she came through the door one evening.

"Well, tell me. It must be good from the way you're smiling."

"In the dream I saw myself kneeling down praying and crying. Then a Voice spoke to me and said, 'My child, what are you crying about?'

"I replied to the Voice, 'My dad and mom are going out to start a church and they have no one to sponsor them and no church to help them. I'm very concerned about them. They don't have enough help.'

"The Voice of the Lord spoke to me again so reassuringly, 'My child, don't worry. I'm going to give them five families to start with. Furthermore, I will give your father the gift of wisdom.'"

As she described her revelation, joy filled my heart and I hugged her. It seemed that once again, as soon as I asked, God had given me the answer. He was going to allow me to be the shepherd of His flock in Murlin Heights. His lost sheep were to come from varied backgrounds of religious faith, environments and stations in life. I would discover that some were sick and needed healing, some were wounded and needed binding, some were blind and needed vision restored, and others had been fleeced and needed to be clothed with love.

The future was to reveal that my success as a pastor was not to rest on my feelings about my own abilities, but was to depend entirely on the anointing of the Lord.

Chapter Nineteen

THE "CRISCO" KID

The following Thursday evening, July 27, 1965, without any advertising, except the sign on the front lawn, the doors were opened for the first service. Seventeen souls gathered to worship that memorable night. Excluding Beulah and myself, the congregation consisted of five families. This was the beginning.

A sense of longing to visit my good old daddy pervaded my heart. I so wanted his blessing upon my work. It would mean so much to me to have this seasoned veteran of the gospel lay his hands on me and bless me as Jacob blessed all twelve of his sons.

On a previous trip, I had told him of my call to the ministry. That was before I knew that I would become a pastor. His only words of advice then were that I make certain that what I was doing was the leading of the Lord.

Now I sat facing him, describing the ways

God had blessed me in my new endeavor and about the people he had given me to lead. Dad sat with his eyes closed as if weighing the situation, and then he spoke solemnly, "It's a dreadful thing to be a pastor, Cliff. The load is extremely heavy."

He drew from his store of experience examples of heartaches, trials, and disappointments visited upon his ministry. He continued on, however, on a more positive note when recalling past days of victory when souls were saved, bodies were healed, and lives were transformed through his obedience to God.

Mostly, I just listened. But finally, I revealed the motive behind my visit. I compared myself to the prodigal son. For many years I had turned my back on the inheritance gained from his ministry. Now I had returned to ask for his blessing. It was my desire to have the same anointing rest upon my life that had been on his.

Before I left for home, Dad and I knelt to pray.

The arm of the old overstuffed sofa became my altar. Dad prayed facing his rocking chair on the other side of the room.

It was such a thrill to be permitted to pray with Dad one more time. We prayed uninhibited knowing that we were alone in the house. Our voices blended in the harmony of heartfelt prayer to God. Soon Dad fell silent. Words of praise and adoration still poured forth from my lips as I heard faltering footsteps slowly drawing near.

A sweet cool chill caused a shudder to run down my spine and raised goose flesh on my uplifted arms as Dad laid his hands on my head.

"Lord, I've labored in Your Vineyard for years, but, I'm getting old now. I know, Lord, it's about time for me to be called home. Now, Lord, here's my eldest son; he is following in my footsteps. God, I'm asking You to anoint and bless him. Let him take up where I leave off."

He prayed on for some time, but by then I was weeping. Needless to say, that prayer has stayed with me through these years and has been a tremendous source of comfort to me. Dad's blessing was the greatest inheritance that I ever received from him.

A sense of inadequacy made me very self-conscious in my first few attempts at preaching. The faithful believers whom God had sent to labor with us were a great encouragement. They sat facing me at each service smiling their approval, and adding vocal support with an occasional amen. God was good to us and soon began adding to our number. As the flock increased, I felt a greater need for a special anointing to minister to their needs.

In a vision, the Lord blessed me further. I was looking at my hands, and upon examining them, I found that they were leprous.

I spoke two words, "Leprosy depart!"

Instantly my two hands were clean of leprosy. I spoke again, "Now, let the leprosy return."

The leprosy reappeared. I commanded once again, "Now, let the leprosy depart once again."

And it was so. In my vision I leaped into the air and praised God in a heavenly language. "Thank God He has given me a sign and the same gift He gave to Moses," I thought.

As God had given Moses the sign of the leprous hands to convince Moses that he was the chosen leader to deliver the children of Israel out of the bondage of slavery in Egypt, so God was confirming my calling to lead the people He had given me.

Soon after, God gave me an occasion in which to act as a guiding shepherd of His people. One day an elderly sister from our church sat waiting in the doctor's office. A young mother in the same waiting room seemed to be drawn to this snow-haired saint of God.

The young lady approached the elderly saint and stated, "I believe you're a Christian."

"Yes, I am," was the kindly reply as she

responded with her ready smile and twinkling eyes.

The young woman became excited and said, "I believe if I could get a Holy Ghost-filled preacher to pray for me, I would be healed."

"Do you really believe that?" the Christian lady probed.

"Yes, I do. Do you know where I can find one?"

"Of course," was the reply, "my pastor, Brother Snodgrass, is a Holy Ghost-filled preacher. He and his family will be glad to pray for you."

Arrangements were made for them to go to my daughter's home which was a few blocks from the doctor's office. Wanda called me and I arranged to meet them all there. When our friend arrived with the young lady, we found a soul that desperately needed help and deliverance. At that time, she was paying seven dollars daily for medicine and injections to maintain some sense of tranquility.

She was the troubled victim of three previous nervous breakdowns and had spent periods of time in a mental institution. The members of her own family lived in constant apprehension for her. She was not trusted to keep her baby for fear she would try to destroy it. More than once she had attempted suicide. Even as we sat talking with her, we noticed fresh wounds marking her wrists from a recent attempt to take her life.

Relying on God for wisdom we talked and prayed with her. Before she left the house, we asked that she come to Sunday service the next morning.

We wondered what her behavior would be in church, for until now no one had been able to control her. The evil spirits, which in the past had raged within her, seemed subdued as she sat and received the Word of God that morning. At the close of the service, I asked her to come forward to let us pray with her.

As I laid hands on her, my wife and daughter stood on either side of her and the church agreed with us in prayer.

Our voices filled the small sanctuary as we reached out to the Prince of Peace to bring His peace to that tormented soul. Immediately, several demons, including a suicide spirit, fled from her, screaming with loud voices. As she writhed and struggled, Beulah and Wanda were hardpressed to restrain her.

Soon her body relaxed. The dark expression left her countenance. A smile came over her face revealing quite a beautiful girl. Tears of joy sparkled in her eyes and streamed down her face as she realized that she was finally free from the tormenting powers of darkness. Oh, how good God was to her that morning. Never again was she to be torn inside by the power of Satan.

The following evening, Beulah and I went to

her house. As we entered the modestly furnished living room, we noticed that everything was neat and clean, for she had a new interest in her home. We were amazed at her changed personality. While we were talking an aunt came in. She lived in a small dwelling behind the young girl's house. We continued sharing about Jesus Christ. Seeing the aunt's receptive attitude, we asked if she would consent to pray and give her heart to the Lord.

She spoke up, "Yes, and I've been sick. I need healing, also."

After she confessed her sins to God, we laid our hands on her forehead and agreed together in prayer for her healing. Immediately she exclaimed, "Praise the Lord! The pain is gone!"

She was very excited. "Wait a minute. I've got a sister I want you to pray for."

Out the back door she ran. The young lady explained that the sister lived in an apartment upstairs.

In a few minutes she returned, bringing in tow not only another lady, but a gentleman also. A stroke had left this other aunt's shoulder crippled with an afflicted arm that was drawn backwards and immobilized. The right side of her mouth was drawn down and impaired her speech. Her husband suffered with heart trouble and high blood pressure.

"I want you to pray for my sister and brother-in-law," the woman said, breathless from her mad dash up the stairs. "I was just telling them I got healed."

"Do you want to be prayed for?" I asked, looking directly at them, searching their faces to make certain it was also their desire.

"Yes," they both responded.

I spoke to them of salvation and then read to them from James 5:14-15, "Is there any sick among you? Let him call for the elders of the church; and let them pray over him, anointing him with oil in the name of the Lord:

And the prayer of faith shall save the sick, and the Lord shall raise him up; and if he have commited sins, they shall be forgiven him."

"That's what I want. I want to be anointed with oil," the gentleman responded.

"Do you have any oil?" I asked the young lady of the house.

"I'll go see if I can find some," she replied.

Beulah offered to go with her to help her look. In the meantime, I continued exhorting the others.

On the way to the kitchen, Beulah asked, "Do you have any olive oil?"

"No."

"Any Wesson oil?"

"No."

"Here's some Crisco," the young lady volunteered. "Could you use that?"

To satisfy the request of the couple to be anointed with oil, Beulah took the Crisco and melted a little on the stove.

She soon returned with the oil and we anointed the aunt with it first. Immediately her afflicted arm thrust upward testifying to her healing.

Then, again using the dab of Crisco, we anointed her husband and God honored our simple act of faith. He, too, testified he had experienced divine healing.

The young lady spoke up, "I want you to come over here and pray for my baby."

Earlier, we had noticed a crib in the corner of the room with a small child resting in it. But now as we walked over to it we viewed a pitiful sight. The baby lying there was deformed, its body bowed backwards. A small sad face stared back at us suspiciously.

We anointed the baby with that same Crisco oil and prayed. His small body did not show immediate results from our prayers, but a change took place in his countenance. Fear left his face and a sweet smile shone brightly. From that moment he began improving.

Just recently I saw him. Tears came to my eyes as this young boy stood before me normal and erect.

Through these several healings on that one evening, three families were added to our church. They continued to worship with us until they moved to their native state, taking their testimonies with them.

Chapter Twenty

BURNING BRIDGES

When approximately one year had passed, the need for the church to have a full-time pastor began to weigh heavily on my mind. I wrestled with the decision for some time. The small congregation could hardly afford the loss of the tithe that I was putting into the treasury, let alone adding my weekly salary to the burden.

In a board meeting, while discussing the need for additional space for our growing congregation, the subject of a full-time pastor was interjected by one of the board members. I confessed to them that I was seriously considering making the move, but did not want to go ahead of the Lord. I promised them that I would earnestly pray about the matter.

Once again God opened my understanding and sealed my instructions while my head lay upon the pillow that night.

A long line of people stood in single file

waiting to be prayed for by a certain man of God. This was a man whom I had greatly admired in the early days of my Christian experience. I was standing to his left hoping to be of some assistance. As each person attempted to reach the evangelist, they were hindered by pie racks which were stacked full of the pies that I was selling.

"I'll move these pies out of the way, so that the people can get through," I said apologetically to the evangelist.

"That will be fine, brother," was his reply.

Moving the first rack of pies over to one side, I turned back to get another, but found a rack setting in the same spot as the first. I moved it also. Turning around again there in the same place was still another rack of pies. I worked fervently but always with the same results.

The people were prevented from getting through to the evangelist to be healed.

The very next morning I went into my supervisor's office. I voiced my appreciation for their kindness to me during the years I had worked for them, but I stated that I was giving them my resignation so that I might become a full-time pastor.

I am sure some thought that I was making a foolish mistake, but I was convinced that this was God's time.

A seemingly unimportant decision was required of me as I left the Bluebird Pie

Company that last day. With only six years to go before retirement, I had the opportunity of obtaining a withdrawal card from the union with a fifty cent fee which would have permitted me to retain my seniority for two years in the event that I chose to return to my job.

This would have entitled me to a retirement income of two hundred dollars per month in addition to Social Security benefits. I refused to entertain the temptation to sign the card because I was thoroughly determined to burn all bridges behind me and trust in the Lord completely. Not once have I regretted making that decision because the Lord has proven faithful in every circumstance.

A meeting of the church board of trustees was called to inform them of my decision. One generous board member moved to begin paying me a salary of one hundred and twenty-five dollars per week, the same amount I received from my full-time job with the bakery.

Knowing this would strain the budget while involved in a building program, I declined. I agreed to accept seventy-five dollars per week as a starting salary.

As a full-time pastor, I was able to devote myself more fully to the spiritual needs of the congregation. And, I now had more freedom to begin actively planning for the construction of a new sanctuary.

We were bursting at the seams as new members were added. One night, eighty-nine souls jammed the tiny building. We wondered if the old floor would support so much weight. The automobiles parked haphazardly in the inadequate space outside incurred the wrath of our antagonistic neighbor who blocked the driveway with his car and called the sheriff.

Most of the members were just the kind of people that I had prayed for prior to my becoming a pastor. They were the unwanted and unloved castaways from others churches. And I was truly blessed by the Lord's faithfulness in answering my prayer.

But, even though our number was increasing, it was disturbing to realize that no one had actually been born again under my ministry for some time.

Chapter Twenty-One

HUNGRY

"I'll go hungry until next Sunday night," I declared emphatically to Beulah as we sat facing each other in the breakfast booth in our kitchen having our usual Sunday night after-church snack. "It's been ten months since we've had anyone saved in church," I lamented.

"Are you sure you can make it seven days?" she inquired sympathetically.

"All I know is, I have to do something," I returned.

We continued talking at length about men of God whom we knew or had read about who had reached a certain point in their ministries when they realized their need for the power of God. Almost without exception, we concluded that each had made sacrifices which included much prayer and fasting.

To decide to fast was no easy decision for me. I have always enjoyed eating, and the early training of my childhood years to eat everything on my plate had taken its toll on my waistline. With the exception of the time in which I had lost thirty-five pounds in thirty-five days after the scare concerning my heart condition, I've always had a more than adequate mid-section.

But, my decision to attempt a seven day fast was made out of sheer frustration and desperation. God had to move. A ten month spiritual drought in which not one soul had been born again in the kingdom of God seemed to be a real challenge to the validity of my call to the ministry. Though discouraged, I was still convinced that it was God who had sent us to Murlin Heights to pioneer a church for Him.

Surprisingly, during the following week, the Lord gave me the necessary strength to accomplish each task which presented itself. I'm not saying it was easy, but my hunger for the power of God exceeded my hunger for natural food. The third day proved to be the most difficult as the gnawing hunger within me cried out for gratification. Calling on the Lord for help while summoning every ounce of will-power and self-control, I passed the crisis of that day's craving for food.

That night, Beulah had a vision. When I arrived home the next afternoon from a hard day of work, she revealed the details of her vision to me.

"Listen to what God showed me last night. I don't understand it, but here's what I saw. I looked into a huge tank of water, approximately nine feet long, which was divided into three compartments. I reached into the first compartment to get a drink, but saw that the water was polluted and unfit for drinking. I then reached toward the second compartment. Though the water was not as dirty as the first it was still unclean.

"Finding the water clear in the third compartment, I reached down to get a drink, lapping like a dog from my hand. It was then that I looked and saw a man coming toward me. He appeared to be very frail and sickly. He was just skin and bones.

"I looked into his thin face and noted that he was unshaven as though he had three or four days growth of a salt and pepper grey beard. Without speaking a word, he climbed into the compartment of clean water and sat down looking toward me with a very determined countenance. At that point my vision ended."

I commented that I didn't understand it and cut the conversation short because it was Thursday and I had to catch a nap before conducting the service that evening.

It seemed that I had barely laid down when Beulah awakened me to come to the phone. It was my mother.

"Cliff, there's a man that lives down the

street named Burl Lewellyn. He's really sick and it looks like he might by dying. I was wondering if you could come and pray for him."

"Why sure, Mom," I replied, "but, you would have to find out if they want me to come."

Mom promised that she would inquire and let me know right away. Shortly the phone rang and she had her answer, "He says you can come over and pray for him."

We knew we'd have to hurry in order to get back in time for church, so Beulah and I left immediately.

We were received into the home by Mrs. Lewellyn who took us upstairs into the middle bedroom. There in that dimly lit room was the pitiful sight of a very sick man. The pain in his stomach had caused him to draw his emaciated body into a fetus-like position. His face was gaunt and unsmiling. A heavy growth of beard added grotesquely to his features. His hollow, sunken eyes spoke of much suffering.

"That's the man! That's the man I saw in my vision!" Beulah exclaimed in a low voice.

The traditional pastoral introductions and greetings were exchanged. Then I approached the real reason for our being there.

"Mr. Lewellyn, are you a Christian?"

"No, sir."

"Would you like to be?" I asked.

His response was affirmative. I then turned to his wife asking her if she too would like to accept the Lord Jesus Christ into her heart. She also expressed a desire to be a Christian. I turned to the third chapter of St. John and read the story of Nicodemus, explaining that "you must be born again."

We prayed a brief prayer and then I asked them to repeat after me the "sinner's prayer."

"Dear God, forgive me of my sins. I'm sorry for every sin that I have ever committed. I ask You to wash all my sins away by the cleansing power of the blood of Jesus. I promise by Your help I will live for You all the days of my life. I accept Jesus right now as my personal Savior. Amen."

The prayer was simple and to the point and our visit was shortly terminated. Beulah and I took mother with us and went on to the Thursday night service.

Not having had the benefit of formal training, I relied upon the information gleaned from a book which I had purchased describing proper pastoral etiquette. The book stated that when you pray with a new convert in their home, you wait two days and pay another pastoral visit.

The desire to be a good pastor was uppermost in my mind. So, the following Saturday evening, just two days later, while making my pastoral rounds I arrived at the Lewellyn home.

Sister Lewellyn graciously received me and escorted me to her husband's bedroom. The weakness from my sixth day of fasting made climbing the stairs more tiring than usual.

I was led again down the hall to the third door which was standing open. The scene was unchanged from two days before. The same frail shell of a man still lay doubled on the bed, his knees drawn against his chest because of the unabating pain in his stomach. He had been lying in this position wasting away for the greater part of the last six weeks.

When first afflicted by the sickness, Burl had attempted to keep working. Day after day just after having eaten lunch, he would have to go aside and regurgitate. Finally, after several weeks of taking in so little food to sustain his body, he had taken leave of his job as labor foreman.

Now, he lay helpless. His pallid skin was draped pitifully over his protruding bones. His body had grown so weak that crawling to the bathroom was the only time he left his bed. Just that day, my mother had brought Burl a pint of half and half milk from her little grocery store for him to drink. Just as the baby food which his wife tried to feed him, the milk stayed in his stomach a very short time.

As I entered the room and viewed the heartrending sight, I was moved with compassion. I drew near and asked, "Brother Lewellyn, how are you today?"

"Not good," was his feeble reply.

"I thought I would come and pray for you."

"I'd sure be glad if you would."

I prayed a short prayer, but nothing happened. Then the Spirit spoke to me, "Get down on your face."

I hesitated. The book on pastoral etiquette contained no such instructions when visiting the sick.

"Get down on your face," the Voice once again urged.

"All right, Lord," I quietly yielded.

As I prostrated myself face down upon the throw rug beside Brother Burl's bed, I began to pray. Praying was difficult at first as it seemed I could feel Burl's eyes staring at me in amazement at such a ridiculous act. The back of my neck grew red hot from the heat of embarrassment. Continuing on in prayer I soon overcame my self-consciousness and began to talk to God in earnest.

Then the same Voice which commanded, "Get down on your face," now instructed, "Get up and lay hands on him."

Rising to my feet I stood beside the bed. Brother Lewellyn was lying on the edge of the bed facing me. I turned my face upward, closed my eyes, and reached out with my right hand to touch him. As I raised my left hand, I began to pray. I knew immediately that I had made contact with God, for His power and anointing surged through my body and out through my hand now resting on Brother Lewellyn's head.

"Fire! Fire!" he exclaimed. "I feel fire!"

His knees which had been drawn against him for so long straightened out as he, with the same motion, sat upright in bed. I knew that he had felt that same surge of power that I had.

"How do you feel, brother?" I inquired excitedly.

"I don't know." He was awestricken. "I feel so light. I feel like a feather. You could just blow me away."

"What did you feel at the moment that God touched you?" I questioned.

"I felt fire. It was like electricity that hit me in the top of my head as you laid hands on me and it ran through my body and out the bottom of my feet. It was just like sticking my finger in an open light socket."

I could tell by his changed countenance that something extraordinary had happened.

We rejoiced at the presence of God in that little room.

"I'm hungry," Brother Lewellyn volunteered shortly. "I think I would like to have some buttermilk."

This was the first time that Brother Lewellyn had felt hungry for many days. He drank the milk. This time his stomach didn't reject it.

At 2:30A.M. the next morning, the hunger pangs interrupted Brother Lewellyn's sleep. Quietly he tiptoed downstairs and into the kitchen for a raid on the refrigerator. After satisfying his hunger, he went into the bathroom, where he shaved and showered. Then he returned to bed much refreshed.

The following Monday morning he checked into the Veteran's Administration Hospital because of a previous appointment and weighed in at ninety-four pounds which were distributed skimply over his five foot, eleven inch frame.

After undergoing several inconclusive tests, he was sent home for the Christmas holidays. On January 4, he returned after being informed by the doctor that only surgery would reveal the source of his illness.

"You either have several large ulcers or a tumor or cancer. We will have to perform an exploratory operation to find out."

Several x-rays were taken prior to the scheduled operation and much to the amazement of the physicians they found no trace of the growth that had appeared on the previous x-rays.

Several other tests were performed with the same conclusive results, that the growths had disappeared.

"All we can find is some scar tissue where the growth used to be," was one doctor's remark.

Returning home February 1st, he was called back to work two days later. That healing miracle is still good to this day.

Chapter Twenty-Two

AN "OSCAR" FOR THE CHURCH

"What will your husband say about your getting saved tonight?" I asked Bernice as Beulah and I drove her home from church that evening.

"Oh, he'll get saved too," was her immediate reply.

"What's your husband doing tonight?" I asked.

"He went over to a friend's house and they're probably playing cards. But I know he'll get saved. We've both been under conviction and he's just been waiting on me to make the first move."

Bernice had come to our little church on my mother's invitation. Mom witnessed to nearly everyone she met. She was sitting on the porch when Bernice passed by going to visit a neighbor next door. Mom told her that she had a son who was just starting a new church and invited Bernice to go along with her. She had attended the Sunday morning service and then Sunday night committed her life to God.

Later that week, I made a pastoral call at the new convert's home. There I met her husband for the first time.

"I'll be in church Sunday morning," he promised as I was leaving.

The following Saturday, Beulah and I chanced to meet him in a shopping center near the Kroger store where Beulah was employed as a cashier.

"I'll see you tomorrow morning, preacher," he promised. "I didn't have anything but work clothes to wear so I thought I'd buy a new coat to wear to Sunday School."

We were beginning to believe that he was serious, but decided to just wait and see. What we didn't know was that earlier that same day, he had made an important decision.

As he sat in the old garage of one of his drinking buddies, he looked across the table at the wrinkled face of the eighty-three year old poker player who sat studying his cards.

"You ought to be talking to this old man about his soul instead of sitting here trying to take his money away from him," his conscience seemed to say.

He shoved his beer can back, stood to his feet, threw down his cards and said, "Boys, this is the last time you'll ever see me here."

Naturally, this abrupt interruption of the

card game brought a puzzled response from the three men still sitting at the table.

"I'm a-gonna quit this foolishness, go to church, get saved and go to preachin'," he announced emphatically.

When Sunday morning came, Bernice was there with her husband in his new coat. With Sunday School finished, the song leader was barely into the opening congregational song. The people stood, clapping their hands and singing joyfully, "We shall see the King, we shall see the King, we shall see the King when he comes..."

Heads turned, eyes stared in disbelief at the commotion in the second row. A young red-haired man was caught up in the rhythm of the song as he began to stomp with both feet. His hands waved in the air. Tears streamed down his freckled cheeks. His upturned face seemed to radiate. Words couldn't express the joy that he felt. He just opened his mouth wide and sounded like a freight train as he shouted, "Whoooooooooooo!" following each phrase of "Praise the Lord!" "Halleujah!" "Thank You, Jesus!"

From this moment, Bernice's red-haired young husband began to grow spiritually. Little by little, he began to surrender his life with its old habits to God. He became a real blessing to the church and soon gained the nickname of "Sparkplug," because of his ability to testify with so much enthusiasm that it would ignite the church with pentecostal fire.

"Brother Snodgrass," Bernice stated a while later, "I know that my husband is really saved now. Before he started praying, he used to cuss and yell in his sleep at night. Now all he does is praise the Lord."

He had such simple faith and seemed to easily grasp spiritual truths.

Then in early January, 1966, this faith was tested. For three months a constant severe burning sensation in his stomach accompanied by frequent vomiting led him to consult a physician. The doctor ordered him hospitalized immediately for tests. After almost a week in the hospital, as I stood beside his bed making my daily visitation, the doctor walked in.

"Mr. White," he began, "I have some bad news to tell you. Your tests have revealed several serious problems. Evidently, you are a stone grower. You have gallstones and kidney stones. You also have three big ulcers and they're whoppers," he said as he formed a circle with his thumb and middle finger to show the approximate size.

"Now we aren't worried about the stones and the ulcers, we can take care of those by surgery. What has us concerned is that you have been passing blood in your urine. Although the x-rays have shown nothing on the outside, we believe that you have a tumor in your bladder or several in your kidneys. We need to look further into this. There is a forty percent chance that there is a tumor, and if there is a tumor, there is a one hundred percent chance that it is malignant."

As the doctor continued on with his sobering verdict, he finally said, "What we want is permission to do a laparotomy."

"What does that mean?" Mr. White asked.

"Well, in simple terms, we want to do some plumbing on you. We need to run a tube through your abdomen with a light on the end that will show us pictures of your insides."

"Will it hurt?"

"Well, we will have to make a small incision," was the doctor's reply.

"You boys ain't gonna cut on me," he retorted. "I'm trusting in a high'r pow'r."

"So am I, Mr. White. But don't you believe that higher power gives doctors the wisdom to operate?" the doctor asked.

Finally, the young man signed the papers granting permission for the surgery. The doctor had barely left the room when the patient turned to me and spoke dejectedly, "I wish I hadn't done that. I want to trust God for my healing."

"Do you want me to go get the doctor?" I asked hesitantly.

Here was a man converted under my ministry who was putting into practice what I had been preaching, but it was *my* faith that began to waver. "Now, Brother White, it might be good to know what is wrong. Are you sure you don't want to go through with it?"

"I'm shore," was his positive response.

On my way out of the hospital, I met with the doctor and told him about Mr. White's decision not to have the surgery.

"Well," the doctor replied, shaking his head, "I've seen his kind before. I'll let him go home now, but he'll be back in a few days."

Later in the day, when informed of the decision, Brother White's sister-in-law heard the doctor say, "His condition is like walking around with a loaded gun pointed at his head."

The phone rang at my home that afternoon. Bernice White called to say that her husband was being dismissed from the hospital and asked if I would go get him for her.

"Of course," I replied, "I'll bring him home shortly."

I arrived to find him in his room, dressed, with his suitcase packed. As we exited from the hospital parking lot, he broke the silence, "Brother Cliff, when a man gets saved, he starts acting like he's saved, don't he?"

"I guess that's right," I agreed.

"So," he reasoned, "if a man gets healed, he ought to act like it too, shouldn't he?"

"Yes, that makes sense," I responded.

"Then let's stop somewheres 'n eat."

I was amazed at his bold decision, but decided now was as good a time as any for a test of faith. We pulled into a large restaurant parking lot and went in and took a seat at the counter.

Completely ignoring the bland diet which the doctor had prescribed, he ordered. "Give me a bowl of chili, a hamburger, an order of french fries and a Pepsi."

After devouring that, he ordered pumpkin pie for dessert. I watched him in astonishment. There seemed to be no ill effects from all the grease and spices. No, not until this day. That simple act of putting faith to the test produced healing. His weight increased from a skinny one hundred forty-six pounds to a husky two hundred pounds. Later he underwent a thorough physical examination before being accepted for employment at a large corporation, and was given a clean bill of health.

God was good to us in giving this young man to our church. His life is a continuous testimony of his devotion to Jesus Christ. Our services are greatly enriched whenever he stands to testify in his zealous manner, flavored heavily by the accent which reflects his birthplace, the little community of Hazard, Kentucky. Whenever he enters the building, it's like a "little bit of sunshine" coming in.

In the movie industry, Oscar awards are made each year for outstanding performers and performances. God was pleased and gave us an award that we are thankful for to this day. He gave us an Oscar——Oscar White.

Chapter Twenty-Three

GROWING PAINS

Now that the task of building a new sanctuary lay ahead, the need for finances was uppermost in my mind. We had accumulated $3,000 in our treasury, but knew that this was a small portion of the actual amount needed. Each member of the board, along with Beulah and I, agreed to contribute one thousand dollars apiece to begin building.

With that, the construction began. The first days work stripped away the front porch with its sign marking the old church entrance. The sod then began to feel the bite of the backhoe as great gulps of earth were removed to form a trench for the footer and foundation of the envisioned sanctuary.

I really worked for that seventy-five dollar-a-week salary the church paid me. In addition to being pastor, I became ditch-digger, hod carrier, brick mason, carpenter, plumber, electrician, errand boy, etc.

We continued worshiping in the small building and each Saturday evening following an exhausting week of laboring on the new addition, the task of cleaning up the sawdust and mud which had been tracked through the old auditorium became my job.

Other men of the church who labored with us soon discovered talents and abilities which they had not been aware that they possessed. They also became aware of muscles which had long been unused, but reaffirmed their presence by cramps, aches, and pains.

Soon the walls went up, the trusses were set in place, and we were ready for the roofing.

One day, Brother White braved the cold, early spring chill to assist the laying of the sheeting for the roof. Being unaccustomed to working at such heights, he cautiously maneuvered about fearing that he would slip and tumble from the roof.

Observing the contractor, who himself was a minister, busily working below on the flooring, Brother White called to him, "Brother, I'm scared up here. Will you pray for me?"

"Certainly," and with that the good brother doffed his cap, bowed his head and prayed, asking that God would protect His servant while he worked on the roof.

Brother White proceeded with the assurance that God would watch over him. (I was amused later to find that for added security Brother White had tethered himself with a half-inch rope!)

Each day I was delighted with the progress, for soon we would have accomodations for more classrooms and larger crowds and our building would have the appearance of a church instead of a cottage.

We completed the new sanctuary and moved into it in late spring. The twenty-seven foot wide by forty-one foot long dimensions seemed to be a very spacious auditorium in comparison to the cramped quarters to which we had become accustomed. In our eagerness to worship in the new addition, we could not wait for the pews to be delivered, so in the first few services we used whatever seating was available. We used our old theatre seats, folding chairs, and homemade benches. Some even brought lawn furniture to accomodate the crowds.

Prior to dedication day, I called Brother Claude Ely, minister and gospel singer, to confirm his scheduled revival which was to be the first in our new sanctuary. At that time, he was conducting a revival in Xenia, Ohio. I asked if I could come and get him and bring him to Murlin Heights to see our new addition.

I was like a proud new father. As we rode together in the car, I began to pour out the story of how God had led us in the establishing of our church in Murlin Heights.

Upon arriving, Brother Ely voiced his approval as he surveyed the product of our labors. After touring the inside of the building with its new floors, pecan paneling and freshly painted Sunday School rooms, we walked around the outside of the building.

Before going out, I had mentioned the difficulties we had had with our next-door neighbor to Brother Ely. How from the very beginning he had not ceased to vex us, and continually grew worse.

Recently he had become enraged at those who parked too close to his property line. He warned me that he would be sitting at his kitchen window with a shotgun resting at his side to take care of any trespassers.

"Brother Clifford, the Lord is going to give you that property," Brother Ely stated.

At first I didn't know whether he was prophesying in the Spirit or if he just felt a hunch.

"Don't you do anything about it," he continued. "Just make sure that you deal through a realtor. God is going to give it to you."

We went inside the church once again. Brother Ely seemed to be in a reflective mood. Walking over to the side door, he peered through the small diamond-shaped window that looked out onto the adjoining property. Following a brief pause, he restated his previous prediction, promising that the Lord would give us that property. I accepted it then as being a prophecy from God. It would take a miracle. The lot was zoned for business, besides having three houses and a garage. The price for such a choice piece of real estate would be out of reach for a congregation as small as ours.

Chapter Twenty-Four

SUFFERING LITTLE CHILDREN

Bob and Marsha West began attending our church in July, 1967. Along with their four other boys, they brought with them their three-week-old baby, Greg.

Time was given for special prayer during the service.

"I want to have my baby prayed for," Marsha stated as she presented him at the altar.

"I want God to give him a breastbone."

When the baby was first born, it was discovered that he had no sternum or breastbone. There was a gap between the ribs in front which created a depression in his chest.

There was no dramatic change from our prayers that night.

Soon cold weather arrived, and without this natural protection in his chest the baby got pneumonia which kept him hospitalized from November to February.

During that time, the doctors took tests on baby Greg and added another startling report, "the child is also mentally retarded."

As soon as he came home from the hospital, back to church his mother brought him, with a renewed determination that God was going to heal her baby. She never seemed to weary.

Each week she took him to the hospital for a checkup and each week the church prayed for him.

Several months of prayer had passed when one day Sister West was changing Greg's clothes. She laid him back to put on an undershirt when she noticed his chest was no longer sunken in. Quickly examining him she found that there seemed to be a hard surface beneath the skin.

She made an appointment with the doctor to have him x-rayed. The doctors soon confirmed that the bone had indeed begun to grow.

God used this miracle to draw many friends of the West family into the church and add to our congregation. But there were still other things God needed to do for that child.

Soon after he began to talk, the family noticed he had a speech problem. Again he was taken to the specialist who confirmed this and repeated the earlier finding that he was indeed mentally retarded.

His mother again presented him to God for a complete healing. His speech began to improve, although it did not correct itself instantly.

Now he is in his first year of school and the doctors have declared that there is no evidence of mental retardation.

His first grade teacher called Sister West at the beginning of the school year to tell her there was absolutely no evidence that he had even *had* a problem with his speech.

While writing this book, God wonderfully filled little Greg West, now eight years old, with the baptism of the Holy Ghost.

It had been nearly ten years that the Lord had been blessing me with dreams and visions, and on quite a number of occasions, I had felt that supernatural being on my left side. And, as always, when I felt that presence, God would heal someone or perform a miracle.

I knew this supernatural person at my left surely was the angel of the Lord who had appeared to me on Easter Sunday, in 1958. Since I had been permitted to see him twice, I knew very well how He looked. That had never left my memory.

When this amber-colored "man" made his presence known, I could always feel the intense heat next to me. It was a source of great comfort to feel him, for then I would know that God was with me.

But, a lengthy period of time had passed in which I had not felt the angel's presence. I was concerned, for I did not want to lose that special anointing.

One day another good Christian brother and I began reminiscing about the past and the outstanding experiences we had had with God. I related to him how it had been some time since I had felt that Divine Presence in the form of heat. The brother agreed to pray and ask that the Lord would restore this anointing to me.

Around four in the morning on November 8, 1968, I came to myself standing in the middle of my bedroom floor with stuttering, stammering lips. Now trembling from head to toe with the anointing, I realized that I had been dancing in the Spirit.

Overcome with what I had seen and heard, I had to wake Beulah, for I felt she surely must have heard me.

"Wake up, honey. Did you hear me singing in the Spirit?"

"No, but I heard you groaning and moaning."

"You'll never believe what the Lord has shown me tonight. It was wonderful. I saw myself opening the Bible to the second chapter of the Gospel of John which tells of Jesus turning the water into wine at the wedding in Cana of Galilee.

"Then suddenly there appeared an angel of

the Lord standing right behind me, who in appearance resembled a well-known evangelist. He reached over my shoulder and pointed his finger to the place near the edge of the Bible where I was reading.

"As He moved his finger down the page, I followed along, reading. He stopped and spoke, 'You must get the key word.'

"I noticed this Bible was different from a regular Bible which usually has black writing on white pages. In this case there was a portion marked on the page which was printed in gold letters on blue paper. I gazed long and hard at the word to which he pointed, but could not read it, neither did I understand it. The word was foreign to me.

"Again the angel spoke, 'This is the key word to the text and each message that you preach will have a key word which must be illuminated by the Holy Spirit.'

"After I read these words, he took out a tuning fork and touched it to my lips. As he touched my lips, a beautiful melody began to pour forth. The words of the song were also in an 'unknown' tongue.

"As I sang, I watched the angel, who was now no longer the size of a man. He had grown and stood with his head reaching into the heaven and with his feet resting upon the earth.

"Still singing, I lifted my hands into the air and looked up. Now I caught sight of what I knew was the river of life. The river was flowing from my left to my right. I stood with it covering my head like a canopy. It seemed as if God had turned it upside down especially for me that night. It was as clear as crystal so I even noticed little pebbles in the moving water.

"As I stood there holding my hands up in worship, the water began to descend over my fingers and hands and run down my wrist. My right hand was completely submerged in the water and as it flowed across it, I could feel it ripple. Although my hands did not get wet, it still felt like water.

"Standing there, I realized that I was still singing in this heavenly language that I had never used before. It took absolutely no effort to sing; the notes were high and pure.

(There is a dear sister in our church, Brenda Mays, who is an excellent singer and can easily hit a C above high C.)

"While I listened to myself, I thought, 'If Brenda could only hear me now. I know I must surely be singing higher than she ever did.'

"I was so thrilled and pleased, for I knew I was singing in a heavenly voice. The quality of every note was perfect.

"I sang on and on for some time, and the realization came to me that my voice was being carried for miles and miles. Then the river began to lift and slowly went back to its original position over my head.

"As I watched it ascending, I noticed a

small whirlpool, and thought, 'If I can just look through that little whirlpool, I can look into the eye of God.'

"Suddenly I came to myself and was no longer singing. Instead, I was standing in the middle of the floor 'groaning in the Spirit,'" I finished.

"That's what I heard," Beulah commented. "I didn't know all the rest of that was going on and I surely didn't hear you singing."

But, I knew that I had been greatly blessed of God. I took this as an answer to the previous night's prayer that God would soon restore my ability to detect the angel of the Lord on my left side. And when he did, I knew miracles would result.

A few days following my vision of the river of life, the Hockett family visited our church. Dennis came first on a Sunday morning and surrendered his life to God at the close of the service.

"I want to get me some of that joy," he had stated to his wife on returning home.

The next week he returned and brought his wife and three boys. Because of her church background, she was apprehensive at first for she had heard nothing but bad reports concerning full-gospel believers. The Spirit of the Lord touched her heart and she gave her life to God.

They both expressed a desire to be baptized

in water, so the following Easter, 1970, they followed the commandment of the Lord in water baptism.

Sister Patsy was so full of the power of God, that before I could even submerge her, she received the baptism of the Holy Ghost.

The thrill of this new life and power with God made their faith high.

"We believe God can heal our son," Sister Patsy declared. She began to tell me about little Timmy, the middle child.

From the time he had been two months old, Patsy had a fear in her heart. One night she heard him in his bed making strange noises from deep in his throat. She ran to his bedside, not knowing what was happening. As she watched the child anxiously, she knew that this was not normal.

As he grew, he became extremely active and required constant attention, for he didn't know the meaning of danger or fear. He climbed everything and would repeatedly hurt or burn himself.

Timmy was taken to a doctor when his mother realized that he wasn't making the progress of a normal three year old. The doctor diagnosed his condition as cerebral palsy. The doctor also stated that he was retarded and would remain so the rest of his life.

He walked on his toes, never flat on his feet. At four and half years old, he had never spoken coherently, but continued to make disturbing sounds. Patsy thought he might have said "bye" and "Dad," but was never sure for these were only guttural sounds.

Up until the time she received salvation, her constant vigil over him had left her in a highly nervous state in which she would often scream in despair when he became too much for her to handle.

Timmy would turn and scream back.

The parents brought that little boy to the Almighty Source for healing. I called the whole church to come and stand behind them as we agreed together that God would undertake for little Timmy.

Several days later, I visited the Hockett's home. Timmy came in from outside where he had been playing in water. When he came in the house, he dropped his wet coat on the floor.

"Timmy, pick up that coat," his mother called to him.

Timmy turned and looked at her.

Again she stated, "Pick up your coat!" Suddenly, Timmy reached down, picked up his coat and took it to his room.

Patsy turned to me with tears in her eyes, "Brother Snodgrass, that is the first time he has ever obeyed me."

A great change took place in Timmy in the next few weeks, and he steadily improved. His speech came to him. In fact, during that first week, he even began singing while he played. He returned to the doctor, who checked him thoroughly and could not find a trace of the former retardation.

Several months later, when he was five, his mother wanted to enter him into kindergarten. He was given a readiness test.

The teacher said, "I'm sorry, Mrs. Hockett, but Timmy is not mature enough for kindergarten yet."

Sister Patsy could not accept this, for he had progressed so noticeably. After further prayer at the church, she returned to the school two weeks later. The teacher changed her mind, "I want to go ahead and put him in kindergarten."

Joyfully, Patsy asked me to observe Timmy, for now he was walking normally.

About a year later, he returned to the doctor for further tests. The palsy had disappeared. Tests were then given to him by a psychologist. It was discovered there was absolutely no retardation, in fact, Timmy had an extremely high I. Q. The doctors were indeed amazed.

A few weeks ago, I passed by the Junior Church and saw Timmy leading the singing. Now he is doing well in school, learning rapidly, and catching up with his class even though he had started out four years behind in his abilities.

These are but a few of the cases of deliverance and healing that continued to take place following our move from the small auditorium into our first addition.

I could not begin to tell them all, but have chosen these because they have been proven beyond doubt and verified by resulting medical tests and serve as examples of God's concern for suffering little children.

Chapter Twenty-Five

THE PROMISED LAND

We were really proud of our little white frame church as it sat with a sandstone front facing out on the busy thoroughfare of North Dixie Drive.

The wooden maroon cross testified to our faith in the atoning work of our Savior. At night it offered comfort to those who passed by and saw the soft light outlining that perfect symbol of God's love for humanity.

The interior had been tastefully decorated and as one inspector said to me upon entering, "How refreshing to see a church so simple and yet so beautiful."

I loved the new church building which the Lord had given us. We had built it to the maximum dimensions allowed by the building code in proportion to the size of the lot.

However, with the exception of the sandstone front, it did not resemble the beautiful edifice I had seen in my initial vision of God's promised sanctuary.

As our membership continued to grow, parking once again became a problem.

At the rear of the church was a lot thirty-three feet wide and one hundred and ninety-eight feet long. As I stood behind the church, I would look at that lot and think, "We certainly need that space for extra parking."

I decided to investigate the matter and called on our friend, Harry Lamb, and asked, "Harry, you know that lot behind our church? Could you find out who owns it? We need it badly for a parking lot, but we can't afford to pay too much for it."

Harry was a trustee for the township at that time. "Sure, I know who owns that land," he said. "He's a good friend of mine. He's a druggist who owns a whole strip of land up to Vandalia. It used to be the old traction line from Dayton to Troy."

"Then do you think he would sell it?" I asked doubtfully after this disclosure, knowing that the owner probably had plans for it.

"Well, Cliff, I'll talk to him and find out," Harry told me.

The next day, Harry sought the owner and told him his purpose for seeking him out.

"This church doesn't have any money," he explained. "Why don't you sell it to them really cheap?"

The man asked, "Do you think they could

pay for the deed transfer taxes if I were to give it to them?"

"Of course, they could," was Harry's astonished answer.

From that point, things progressed so rapidly and miraculously that only God, moving divinely on people's hearts, could have caused the chain reaction that resulted.

Harry insisted on going to the Montgomery County Court House and searching the records free of charge. Then he proceeded to check with a lawyer who lived nearby in the township. Again God moved.

The lawyer stated, "Well, if you are doing your work free for the church, and the other man is donating the property, then I will do the legal work for nothing."

The land was appraised at $1,000, but was of much more value to us than that. God had seen our need and again proved that he indeed had set His approval upon the establishment of a work in Murlin Heights.

And, we were growing. One day in June, 1971, I stood in front of our sanctuary after our third enlargement, and looked south toward the adjoining property which our contentious neighbor owned.

He had continued to be a thorn in our side, and it was becoming increasingly difficult to reason with him.

The time came, however, when our confrontations became less frequent. I began to notice his hale and hearty appearance seemed to fade and shrivel as a flower severed from its stem. He appeared to age ten years in less than a year.

One day, I noticed many cars clustered around his home. I reasoned that they must be having some sort of family gathering. A few days later, I was informed by another acquaintance in the neighborhood that he had passed away.

A short time later I received a phone call. It was the deceased man's wife.

"If you think my husband was hard to get along with, preacher, you're going to find out that I'm twice as mean," she stated hatefully.

We were not to be left without adversity, for immediately his wife took up where he had left off, only with greater zeal.

The mortar in the joints of the foundation of our new auditorium had barely enough time to cure when we had to repair the corner of it where she had driven her car, trying to knock the church down. A neighbor reported that she had witnessed the woman as she repeatedly hammered the building with her automobile. Before the evidence could be brought against her, she bought a new car.

She also resorted to calling the sheriff when a visitor would park unintentionally on her property.

If the service became a bit noisy, she would ring her big dinner bell incessantly to annoy us. Many times she could be observed through an open window gesturing offensively toward the church.

As the pastor, I received the brunt of her attacks which included profuse cursing and crank phone calls.

As I looked upon her land, the Spirit of the Lord reminded me of His promise through Brother Claude Ely that He would give us the property.

"Lord," I began to pray, "I haven't asked for the property before because we have not needed it. But, now we need it. We lay claim to it. Lord, our church is willing to pay this woman a fair price for the property. I don't want You to take it away from her. But, we do want You to deduct from the price the cost of damages that she did to Your sanctuary by driving her car into it, trying to knock it down."

I presented our need to the Lord and waited. Ten days later, I looked out the window to see auctioneers placing signs which announced that the property we had claimed would be auctioned July 9th and 10th.

I stepped out to speak to one of the men, "Are you going to sell the property?"

He replied, "Yes."

I knew that the property was very valuable and I didn't want to lose it. I said to one of the men, "I'll tell you what I'll do right now. We'll just give you $25,000 for it and you won't even have to have an auction." I paused. "We're going to get it anyhow."

He stopped what he was doing and looked at me as if I were crazy. "I'm sorry, but we can't take it; the lady thinks she is going to get $50,000 out of the property. It is very valuable."

"I know it is. I'll see you the day of the auction," I replied as I walked away.

That day seemed to draw close quickly. I knew that God had promised us that property, but our church funds were extremely low. A day or two before the auction, the devil began to tempt me, "You just *think* you are going to get that property. You don't have any money and you're not financially able to get any."

I knew all that, but reminded myself that God had promised this property for the church through prophecy. I said, "God will keep His promise."

Then the devil slipped in one of his sneaky questions, "But, what if it is for some other time?"

I found myself listening to him. Troubled in my mind I went home, and got down on my knees, beseeching God, "Father, is this the time for us to purchase the property, or will it be at a later date?"

Then after retiring for bed, once again I clearly heard the Voice of the Lord, "You are going to get the property at this time. When you do, as a testimony of my work, write a book of the history of the building of this church. Name it, *The Miracle of Murlin Heights*."

I woke up in a state of excitement mingled with anticipation. I knew now what my next steps should be. The prophecy given by Brother Ely had stated for us to deal through a realtor.

I called my friend Harry Lamb once again, "Harry, what would you charge the Lord to do a little work for Him?"

Quickly he replied, "Oh, Cliff, I wouldn't charge the Lord anything."

"Well, I'd like you to have that property next to the church appraised so that I will know how much State Fidelity Savings and Loan will lend me for it. I have a promise from the Lord that we will get it."

"Okay, Cliff, I'll see what I can do."

State Fidelity responded positively. "Harry, you tell that preacher out there to bid up to $40,000. If he needs more than that, we'll help him on it."

When Harry told me, I could hardly believe it. I had never dealt with that kind of money before in my life. It sounded too good to be true. I felt I must check on it myself, for surely there was some mistake. Timidly I went to State Fidelity and asked, "Did you really say that you would give us $40,000 and more if we needed it?"

"Yes, we sure did."

I left there amazed and ashamed. I hated to have Harry know that I was questioning him, but I had to hear for myself. I got into the car and praised the Lord all the way home. I knew He was on the scene and was moving in our behalf.

When auction day arrived, I rose early, unable to sleep and anxious for it to begin. The first day all the household goods and many antiques went on the block. July 9th came and passed. I anxiously asked the church treasurer, "How much money do we have in our treasury anyhow?"

Sister Owens replied, "Forty-nine dollars and eighty-eight cents."

I pondered how God was going to let us buy the property with such a small sum. The contract to close the sale required a $3000 down payment by the highest bidder at once. Then the balance was to be paid within forty-eight hours—and all we had was forty-nine dollars and eighty-eight cents.

A family in the church was about to leave for Florida to visit relatives. They stopped by the house on the way to say goodbye.

"Pastor, we have a little money in our account that you are welcome to use if it would help you buy that property. Here's a signed check. But don't fill in more than three thousand dollars. That's all we have in the bank."

I shouted and danced before the Lord. That

was the exact sum we needed. Oh how I praised the Lord for people like the Strickland family.

The next day dawned and I rose, anxious for the bidding on the property to begin. Roughly $50,000 worth of antiques had already gone under the gavel. As I walked around the property, I saw approximately one hundred people milling around. Many of them were businessmen who were also interested in the grounds. There was a plumbing company who wanted the corner lot, another company wanted to build several apartment complexes. I grew somewhat troubled, "I don't know what I am going to do, but there's one thing about it, Lord, I trust You."

It began to grow dark as clouds gathered overhead. The auctioneers put up a little tent in the back yard. A slight drizzle had begun to fall. I left Harry sitting there under that tent and began nervously walking around in the yard. I had come to a decision. I went and got a small bottle of oil out of the church. I decided, "Well, since I anointed the walnut tree in front of 8921 North Dixie just a few short years ago, I will try that again. God honored it the first time, surely He will again."

The Scripture of God's promise to Abraham came to my mind and kept ringing over and over. "Wherever you walk, wherever you set your foot, I will give you the land."

My eyes scanned the property. It wasn't

very far around that lot; eighty-two and a half feet wide by one hundred and ninety feet long, the description read. I would do it. I got the little bottle of oil and secretly anointed the mailbox. Then I began my trek around the boundaries.

Immediately, I sensed that people were staring at me, wondering what I was doing. I'm sure I made a strange spectacle of myself—walking around out there in the rain.

But I ignored them and went on walking. In my heart, I was praying, "Every time I set my foot down I'm claiming this property in Your name. Because You told Abraham *he* could, God, You told me *I* could. I'm walking around these boundaries claiming it in Your name."

Finally, I came back to where I had started, and went back into the tent. Harry was sitting there to represent us, for he knew how to bid at an auction.

I sat down beside him and he leaned over and whispered to me, "How high can we go?"

Quietly I told him, "We cannot go any higher than $35,000. The church board took a vote last night and will not agree to an amount higher than that."

This was a much lower sum than the appraised value given us of $40,000 and much, much lower than the $50,000 the owner declared she must have. Finally at 3:00 P.M., the auctioneer began describing the property and its valuable merits. As I sat and listened, I noticed the other businessmen listening intently also.

I began praying silently, "Now, Lord, in the book of Zechariah it says, 'Not by might, nor by power, but by My Spirit, saith the Lord of Hosts.' Lord, take Your Spirit and let Him speak to each of these men who have come to bid and tell them that they don't want this property. Close their mouths so they won't bid."

The rapid-fire staccato voice of the auctioneer pierced the damp dreary air, "Ladies and gentlemen, we'll start the bidding at $40,000."

No one opened their mouth. He waited. Finally he dropped back to $35,000. Again there was no bid. He pressured and cajoled the people to bid. Reluctantly, he asked for $30,000.

As he did so, he stated, "I have dropped the price, but I don't think the owner will take it."

I thought to myself, "I'm curious to know how much we'll get it for."

He droned on for some time about the $30,000 price, then finally he asked, "Will somebody make me an offer."

"We'll give you $25,000," Harry responded.

My heart leaped, and welled up in my throat. Another man quickly spoke up, "I'll give $26,000."

I looked around to see who made the bid. I became indignant when I realized it was a friend of the owners who stayed on the property quite a bit. Something inside me said, "This man cannot give $26,000. He's been planted to try and raise the price."

Harry spoke up, "We'll raise to $27,000."

This man spoke up immediately, "I'll give you $28,000."

I began frantically to pray now, "Lord, You must stop this some way."

Harry raised his hand for $29,000. It seemed as if I could hear my own heart beating, waiting in the silence that followed for someone to bid. Finally the auctioneer began, "$29,000 once. $29,000 twice." He paused.

I waited.

"$29,000 thrice. Sold!" He pounded his gavel, "Sold on the condition that the owner will accept it, for it is such an extremely low price."

Quickly I wrote out the sum of three thousand and no one-hundredths dollars on the signed check that Bill and Nina Strickland had left with me.

Even though I had to give the auctioneer $3000 of someone else's money because the church had only $49.88 in its treasury, I felt like I was walking tall. The Spirit of the Lord rested upon me and I began to weep. I had a hard time holding back my tears in front of all those people. God's promises were coming to pass.

The owner, when presented the figures of the auction, stated emphatically that she would not sign. The auctioneer tried to persuade her. But I was positive now that God was with us and He could make her change her mind.

Finally, they gave her until three o'clock Monday afternoon to make her decision. The general comment around us was that she would not agree to it.

The entire church prayed about the matter Sunday and we waited. She was determined not to give us an answer until the final moments of the deadline.

Finally at 3:00 P.M. Monday, we reached an agreement. She signed.

Needing the money within forty-eight hours after the agreement, I called State Fidelity immediately. They had been so kind on previous loans and now proved true to their word. With no time lost, papers were drawn up and a closing was set. Shortly, the money was transferred and the property officially belonged to the First Pentecostal Church of Murlin Heights. *God had performed a miracle.*

We had gained the property, but needless to say, we were really broke now. Not only did we have a new loan from State Fidelity of $29,000, but we still carried a balance of $12,000 on the previous loan. Of course, compared to the value of this property, it was but a drop in the bucket.

Finally, moving day came. To our dismay, after inspecting the three houses we had just purchased, we found the water pipes were frozen in two of them.

The church insisted we make a parsonage out of the larger house, so Beulah and I found ourselves moving into a new home.

We were bone weary that night after completing our move. I was prepared to take a bath, when we discovered that there was not enough water in the well to make more than an inch of water in the bathtub.

Here we were, broke, and needing city water on the property. The next day I called a plumbing contractor for an estimate. We were informed it would cost $700 to have city water installed.

That was quite a blow financially, and then there was still another one to come. Our insurance was due immediately on the new property. Our financial debts due in the next ten days totaled $1,800 which we had not previously planned. It was tempting to tell the congregation of our pressing dilemma. Then I realized that God had always supplied the needs, and never before had we begged for an offering. Each service we simply received what He allowed people to give and always it had been sufficient without begging.

So that following Sunday morning, without having told anyone but Beulah, I said simply, "Now, we are going to worship God with our tithes and offerings."

As a rule, the offerings usually were around $300 a week, but when Sunday's offering was counted we had received twice that amount. Thursday night's offering again was $600, and the same the next Sunday service. I knew that only God could have moved the hearts of the congregation to give the exact sum we needed when they knew nothing about it. How we rejoiced together when I revealed the facts to the congregation at the following service.

As did the Israelites when they entered the Promised Land, we began to move in, build, and possess it. During the course of the next year, we had moved into the parsonage, repaired the two other houses and placed tenants from among the congregation in them.

Then, we began to visit other churches, checking the architectural structure, floor plans and interior design until we decided what pleased us most, for now God had put it on my heart to build the church of my dreams.

But, before building the new sanctuary addition to the south side of the property, there was a sturdily built garage that needed to be moved to another part of the land.

A house moving company was contacted. The work was to be done in two weeks. I waited and waited for the movers to arrive. Finally, after six or seven weeks, I grew discouraged, for the work on the new sanctuary could not begin until this task was first completed.

I prayed and asked the Lord to help us get underway, for each day some member of the congregation would question, "When are they coming?"

I watched as their enthusiasm waned.

Finally, the Lord gave me encouragement in a dream as He had done so many times before. I heard a man's voice speaking to me, "Can I have permission to take a hammer and break off the foundation near the door of the garage? It isn't wide enough to permit our truck with its dual wheels to drive in. Then the truck can pick it up and move it away."

As soon as he finished his explanation, I awoke. I turned to Beulah, woke her and told her my dream. We agreed that the Lord was showing me that the laborers were finally coming.

Not five minutes later, the phone rang. The foreman of the movers asked, "Reverend, how wide did you say your garage is?"

I replied, "Eighteen feet."

"We'll be right over as soon as we throw some timber in the truck."

I could hardly contain myself until he hung up. Then I spent a blessed time in praise, for God had reminded me that He was still directing us every step of the way.

About three hours later, the movers arrived. They began backing the big truck into the garage, but had to stop because the doorway, which was built for a car, was too narrow for the large truck. Soon one of the men came over to where I stood watching.

"May I have permission to take a hammer and break off part of the foundation near the door? The doorway isn't wide enough to permit a truck with dual wheels to drive into the garage."

Trying to keep from smiling because of the dream in which I had heard those exact words, I gave him permission. It didn't really matter, for that concrete was going to be broken up anyway. I had to run back into the house to have another "spell of praise."

Finally, the garage was moved to the rear of the property. We were ready to begin the construction of our new sanctuary. I looked around at what the Lord had given us. I began to comprehend what He meant when He said he would *give* us the property. Previously, I had wondered how he could *give* it to us when we would still have to *pay* for it. Now I understood. The income from the two other rental houses on the property would cover the payments on the newly acquired land which would eventually pay for itself. Since it paid for itself, it was a gift from God.

But the Lord wasn't through. He was soon to add to our recently purchased territories. Between the old parking lot and the new property was the undedicated street extending into our land.

We went to the attorney who had previously

helped us and informed him of our desire to have the street incorporated into the existing properties.

Going to court in our stead, he filed an order to vacate the street, and placed our claim on it. Frontage on North Dixie Drive is worth $500 per running foot. This times thirty-three feet made the net worth of the land around $17,000.

Eight weeks passed. Finally we were called to court. The judge of the Montgomery County Courts signed and handed over the deed which gave us clear possession of a street that had been known as Third Avenue or Kirkland Street. Our total investment for lawyer fees and court costs amounted to ninety-five dollars. This for a property worth $17,000!

God had finally brought to pass the final claim which gave us total possession of all the promised land.

Chapter Twenty-Six

THE MIRACLE

We had no building fund, we never took a "prove me" offering, we never used gimmicks and psychology. We never had a bake sale, cake sale, rummage sale or chicken supper. With only our tithes and offerings for which we never begged, we proceeded to build.

Trusting the Lord to bring to pass the work He had begun, we decided to proceed as far as we could before applying for a building loan to complete it.

Brother Dewey Pope, who is a member of another church, donated his labor and machinery, charging only for the operating expenses. Digging a trench for a footer and foundation with his backhoe, he soon outlined the perimeter of the new sanctuary. Later when an apron of concrete was poured over the entire area between the foundation walls, I was elated. "We'll have plenty of room to shout now," I rejoiced.

Friends and neighbors volunteered their carpentry and plumbing talents. Pastor Ralph McFarland of the Fort McKinley Church of God gave freely of his time to work and fellowship with us.

Finally, we reached the point where we needed large sums of money at a time. I returned to State Fidelity Savings and Loan.

I spoke to one of the directors, "You remarked to me one time that if the church ever needed money to build to come and see you. Well, I'm here."

"Reverend, how much do you need?" he asked.

"I don't really know, I'm not a cost consultant, but maybe $30,000."

"Just write down on this piece of paper what you think you will need."

Quickly I drove back to the church, counted two by fours, sheeting and other things. Having had little experience in building, I figured the cost as closely as I could, and went back to State Fidelity to tell them I needed $32,000.

Asking no questions, they set a closing date a few days later. The pen was passed from one board member and his wife to another. Soon all papers were signed and State Fidelity made the money available to us.

And, people continued to volunteer their labor, men and women as well. Whenever there was a job that needed doing, even if it was just sweeping, somebody was standing by and ready.

Soon the skeleton of our new sanctuary stood starkly beautiful before my eyes. The huge crane which had set the trusses in place was finally gone. The roof and sheeting were installed. When the weather began to get bad, we were suddenly unable to get roofers. Feeling sorry for me when I voiced concern that the rain would harm the plywood sheeting, two of the ladies from the church put on their husband's pajamas under their dresses and climbed on the roof and finished nailing down the felt.

While awaiting completion of the new sanctuary, we began a revival with the Reverend and Mrs. Bill Addis. While working outside one morning, I chanced to glance up. There on the roof was a beautiful snow white dove sitting silently just above the spot where the pulpit was to be. I ran into the house to get my movie camera because the sight was so startling. I returned to find him still sitting there where he remained for an hour or so. I marvelled at the sight, believing that God had given us another sign of His blessing.

I could hardly wait to finish the church. Finally, we were able to set a target date of May 1 for the first service in the new sanctuary. The carpet and pews were due to arrive and be installed by that date. We worked diligently to meet the deadline.

A good pastor friend of mine in Springfield expressed a desire to preach the first sermon in the new church. We began to advertise a few weeks before through a promotion called, "PACK A PEW" Except for special rallies and revivals, we had never had more than one hundred and thirty-one people in our church on Sunday.

The carpet men were late in the installation, and we had to postpone setting up the pews for one more week. So when the moving day arrived, we had one hundred and sixty-eight people to fill the pews but no pews. Though we broke our previous attendance record, the crowd looked very small as the people were scattered throughout the new auditorium which had a seating capacity of four hundred and fifty.

A few short weeks later, we were finally ready for the dedication. We wished to give back to the Lord what He had given us.

I could still hear Brother Claude Ely's words, "Brother Clifford, the Lord is going to give you that property next door."

Here was the promise of the Lord, the miracle come to pass. I felt no other person could be the speaker for that dedicatory service.

My wife and I wanted to tell Brother Ely in person all that had come to pass. We wanted to see his face when we told him. During the week following the first service, we drove to Newport, Kentucky, and visited his home. He had not heard from us since the time he had been in revival in the first sanctuary we had built.

I began to relate all that had happened to him. Finally I stated, "Brother Ely, we want to dedicate that new church now, and we want you to be the speaker."

Tears trickled down his cheeks. He dropped his eyes and bowed his head. "All right," he humbly agreed.

The day we had dreamed of for so long was finally here! On August 12th, 1973, approximately two hundred and fifty joyous people celebrated that momentous occasion with us. God moved tremendously in the service.

I had asked Reverend Vearl Vaughn to be present and receive the offering that day. He said to me, "Sure. What do you need yet?"

I said, "Well, we still need some carpeting for the floor of the old sanctuary. We're using it now for our Junior Church."

"What do you think it will cost you?" he inquired.

"I am not certain," I responded. "I have estimated around $2,000."

On dedication day, as we reviewed the past eight years, I rejoiced at the handiwork of the

Lord. Through four expansion programs our usable floor space had grown from 720 square feet in the little cottage to a spacious 7900 square feet.

That day, we dedicated to the Lord the product of our labor of love. The four-sided hanging light fixtures scattered their brilliance over the congregation as the people sat in comfort on the gold upholstered pews. The cool breeze from the central air conditioning system permitted the worshiper to forget the stifling August heat outside.

The light shining through the amber cross above the baptistry matched the trim on the tops and bottoms of the lantern lights. The windows situated on either side of the exposed walnut stained beams were also amber.

As I sat with visiting ministers in the front row of the choir, my eyes strained against the bright spotlights which illuminated the three-tiered elevated choir with its blocks of walnut paneling. I looked with love and appreciation upon the beautiful group of fellow Christians who came to share this sacred time with us. All were visible because of the elevated floor.

As Brother Vaughn stood to receive the offering that day, he told the people, "This will be a free will offering to complete the work on this church. I myself will start off by giving the first one hundred dollars."

God moved on the hearts of the good people

in attendance and within minutes we had received twelve hundred sixty-one dollars and ten cents.

Eager to put God's money to work, I called a carpet store the next morning. The salesman came out, measured the floor and stated, "The final price will be twelve hundred fifty-eight dollars and ten cents."

Again, God had supplied the needed money with three dollars left over.

God's approval was upon the service that day. Following a special song by our realtor Harry Lamb and his wife Alta, an anointed message was delivered by Reverend Claude Ely.

With his guitar hanging about his neck, Brother Ely stepped to the microphone his face beaming, his broad toothy smile as always emphasized by a single gold tooth.

He strummed the guitar once to set the pitch of the song. Then he broke forth in his heavily accented Virginia voice with one of the songs he had written "God understands. He knows all about me..."

There is no warming up for Brother Ely; he starts the first note singing with all his might. As he stood before the audience with his feet planted slightly apart, he leaned back away from the microphone and lifted his eyes toward the ceiling. His baritone voice rasping from many years of hard preaching.

The audience sensed his sincerity and was easily led into a more worshipful attitude in preparation for the sermon which would follow. The Holy Spirit had brought a oneness to the worshipers as Brother Ely sang. After laying aside his guitar and discarding his coat, Brother Ely laid his Bible on the pulpit and read from Acts, "Such as I have, give I thee." Those words expressed the feeling of all who had had a part in the building where we now sat worshiping. All the many hours required for its construction, all the sacrifices which had been made, all the energy which had been expended, we were asked to give to God. And we did just that. We had done our best and we were justly proud. But such as we had, we gave unto "Him."

I look often at the blond-colored bricks and stone on the outside of the church and marvel that it is exactly like the vision I had seen in the very beginning, even before we knew the original property was for sale. I have rejoiced many times, dancing on the green carpeting which now covers the floor. The same carpeting that the Lord let me glimpse over eight years before.

At the time of the writing of this book, I still wonder why God chose me to pioneer the church in Murlin Heights. Having had no formal training in the ministry and very little practical experience, he led me through visions and dreams, step-by-step, to the fulfillment of *His* divine purpose. I can truly say with the apostle Paul, "I was not disobedient unto the heavenly vision."

His blessings have continued to be showered upon us as all of our needs have been met. God has sent us Spirit-filled teachers and workers and has supplied for all of our financial situations. In His amazing grace, lost souls have found salvation, sick bodies have been healed, those bound by the powers of darkness have been set free, and many believers have experienced the baptism in the Holy Ghost.

God has truly wrought a Miracle in Murlin Heights!